The Clockwork Soldier
KEN LIU

"Go," Alex said. "If you remember to keep a low profile, neither your father nor his enemies will ever find you here."

The ship had landed in the middle of the jungle, miles away from the closest settlement. Alara was a backwater, barely inhabited, and insignificant to galactic politics. It would take days, perhaps weeks, to walk out of here, stumble into a few colonists, and pretend to be near starvation. Enough time to make up any backstory and make it believable.

Ryder flexed his slender arms and stretched, the movements graceful, dancelike. The strict manner in which he had been bound during the ship's last jump through hyperspace didn't seem to have any lasting ill effects.

He gave Alex a long, appraising look. "What will you tell my father?"

She shrugged. "I'll give him his money back."

"You've never failed before, have you?"

"There's always a first time. I'm human. I'm not perfect." She began to climb back into the ship.

"That's it?"

She stopped halfway up the ladder and looked down at him.

"You don't want to be sure?" he asked, that characteristic smirk playing at the corners of his delicate mouth again. "Don't you want to ask to see me as I really am?"

She considered this. "No. I've already decided to believe you. Trying to make sure can only make things worse. If I find out that you're telling the truth, then I will have ruined this moment, when I can still believe I'm capable of being decent, of trust. If I find out you're lying, then I'll have to consider myself a fool."

"So, again you choose faith before knowledge."

This time, she didn't stop climbing. When she was at the airlock door, she turned around. "Faith is just another name for self-knowledge. You've succeeded, Scheherazade. When you tell your own story, you seize life. Now it's my turn to tell myself a good story, about myself. I know enough. Goodbye."

Ryder watched as the ship rose, shrank, and disappeared into the evening sky. "Thank you," he whispered.

Then he set off into the dark jungle, just another wanderer, a lonely will etching his way across the wilderness.

A few hours earlier:

"The Clockwork Soldier"
A short interactive text adventure by Ryder

You sleep, a smile at the corners of your mouth.

In your dreams, the concentric layers of carp-scale shingles on the Palace's roof reflect the golden light so brilliantly that visitors to Chrysanthemum know right away how the city got its name.

The Princess's Bedroom
You open your eyes and find yourself in bed. The blanket is silky smooth and the mattress soft.

Like most rooms in the Palace, this one is lined with colorful tapestries depicting the heroic deeds of the Hegemons of the Pan-Flores League. Through a narrow slit-window high off the floor, the brilliant morning sunlight diffuses into the room, as does the chittering of birds and the smell of a thousand blooming flowers in the garden. The door to the hallway is closed right now.

Next to the bed is your clockwork soldier, Spring, standing at attention.

> examine soldier

Your faithful companion Spring has been with you as long as you can remember. He's six feet

2

CLARKESWORLD

JANUARY 2014 - ISSUE 88

FICTION

NON-FICTION

Neil Clarke: Publisher/Editor-in-Chief
Sean Wallace: Editor
Kate Baker: Non-Fiction Editor/Podcast Director
Gardner Dozois: Reprint Editor

Clarkesworld Magazine (ISSN: 1937-7843) • Issue 88 • January 2014

© Clarkesworld Magazine, 2014
www.clarkesworldmagazine.com

tall and looks like a living suit of armor. You remember once opening him up when you were younger, and being amazed at the thousands upon thousands of whirling gears and ticking governors and tightly-wound springs inside.

You giggle as you remember the many adventures you've shared together over the years. You've taught Spring everything he knows, and he's saved you from too many scrapes to count.

> get up

You get out of the bed.

> say "hello"

(to Spring)

"Good morning," says Spring. "I know that sometimes you like to go by a different name for fun. What name would you like to go by today?"

(Please enter your name)

> Alex

"Alex it is," Spring says. His voice sounds . . . rusty, lugubrious. He shuffles in place, the gears inside him clanging and scraping against each other. "I'm sorry that I seem to be in a bad mood today."

> ask about mood

"Why are you feeling down?" you ask. A good princess needs to be concerned about the state of mind of her subjects—er, toys.

"I'm not sure. I just feel . . . like a part of me is missing."

"Did a bolt loosen and fall out? Were you not oiled properly? Did I forget to wind you last night?"

"No. It's none of those things. I can't explain it."

> look under bed

A few dust bunnies scurry out of your way.

> look behind tapestries

The walls are made of solid stone. No hidden passages, as far as you can see.

> examine Spring

He looks fine, if a bit morose.

> cheer up Spring

"Why don't we have an adventure today?" you ask. "Maybe we'll find what you want in the rest of the Palace?"

Spring nods. "As you wish."

> exit bedroom

Hallway
The hallway is lit by torches along the wall. To the east is the grand staircase. To the west, some distance down the dimly lit hallway, are two doors.

Spring follows you into the hallway, the loud clangs of his footsteps echoing around the stone walls.

> ask Spring for direction

"You decide," says Spring. "You always do."

> west

Hallway
Spring clangs after you.

> west

Hallway
Spring clangs after you. Then he sighs, sounding like steel wool being rubbed against a grille.

> ask Spring about sigh

"Don't you like following me around?" you ask.

"Following you around today has not activated as many microlevers inside me as usual." Spring pauses, the gears humming and grinding inside him. "I suppose, logically, we can try having me lead instead of follow."

(Allow Spring to lead?)

> yes

"Why do you tantalize me with the impossible?" Spring says. "We both know I can't. I'm an automaton."

Spring shakes his head from side to side, and the loud, grinding noise makes you cover your ears.

"I am so sad that I can no longer move," Spring says.

> examine

The hallway is narrow and windowless but not damp or dark. The torches in the walls provide flickering illumination. The smell of rose otto permeates the air.

> west

Hallway
Spring stays behind, immobile.

> east

Hallway
You see Spring in the middle of the hallway, looking like a heap of rusty metal.

> inventory

You are empty-handed.

> look for oil

There is no clockwork oil in the hallway.

(Come on. First puzzles in interactive text adventures are often easy, but not *this* easy.)

> look for source of rose otto

The fragrance of rose otto permeates the air.

The essence of rose is distilled from the garden outside the Palace by the gardener and his helpers every morning. The Castellan, your father's head clockwork servant, applies it liberally to combat the problem of mildew in enclosed spaces around the Palace. When activated by heat, it can make any place smell fresh and comfortable.

> pick up a torch

You take one of the torches out of the sconces on the wall.

> examine torch

You lean in close to look at the torch, and the fire singes your lovely, chestnut hair.

Spring groans.

> put out torch against the floor

You extinguish the torch. The hallway is now fractionally cooler.

> examine torch

The torch is cleverly designed by the Royal Artificer. The body of the torch is hollow to hold the slow-burning oil, and a smaller compartment near the top holds rose otto.

> get oil from torch

You stick your hand into the hollow body of the torch and . . .

"Ow! Ow!" You hop around. Your hand is covered in hot oil. You're likely to injure your hand if you don't get rid of it quickly.

> apply oil to Spring

You slather the hot oil over the joints in Spring's face and torso.

Spring stands up.

> ask Spring about mood

"You're welcome," you say, since Spring doesn't seem inclined to thank you. That's very uncharacteristic of him, but maybe he's still feeling down.

"Thank you," Spring says. The voice is smooth, but you detect a hint of resentment. "I just wish I had decided to get the oil myself."

"I can order the Royal Artificer to modify your tape and give you the instructions to get oil when you feel rusty," you say.

"That's not what I meant. I wish I had come up with the idea myself. I wish I could punch my own instruction-tape."

Fear, or maybe it's an appetite for thrill, rises in you. "Are you suggesting that you wish to be endowed with the Augustine Module and cross the Cartesian Limit? You know that's forbidden, and any automata found to have crossed the line must be destroyed."

Spring says nothing.

"But maybe what you're missing is a chance to do the forbidden," you muse to yourself.

> west

Outside the King's and Queen's Bedrooms
The door to the King's bedroom (in the northern wall) is made of solid oak. Carved into the door is the figure of a man with two faces—one laughing, one crying. The four eyes on the two faces are inlaid with emeralds.

The door to the Queen's bedroom (in the south-ern wall) is made of pale ash. The figure of a leaping hare is carved into it. Your mother died when you were born, and the room has been sealed off for as long as you can remember. It's too painful for the King to set foot inside.

Spring clangs after you.

8

> north

The door is locked.

> south

The door is locked.

> knock on door to the north.

There is no answer.

Spring shifts his weight from one leg to the other.

"What are you doing?" he asks. "You know the King is away at Wolfsbane for the coronation of Prince Ulu, three days ride away. All the clockwork servants are away to be maintained by the Royal Artificer this morning. You're alone in the Palace."

> kick door to the north.

Ouch! The door barely moves, but you're hopping around on one foot, crying out. Kicking at doors is not something silk slippers are very well-suited for.

A series of metallic clangs come from Spring. You can see he's trying hard to stop his quivering torso.

"Laugh it up," you say, wincing at the pain. "Laugh it up."

> ask Spring to open door.

Spring lumbers into the door, and it smashes into a million little pieces on contact. Where the door used to be there's now just a big hole.

"I had in mind something a little less destructive," you say.

"Just following orders," Spring says.

Alex whirls around in her chair at the beep-beep-beep of the proximity alarm. She sees the slender figure of Ryder in the doorway of the cabin, leaning against the frame.

She's about to apologize for snooping when she notices the smirk on Ryder's face. *Why should I apologize? He's a prisoner on* my *ship.*

She stands up from the chair. "I needed to see what you've been up to on this computer. You've been using it practically nonstop. A security precaution—I'm sure you understand."

He comes into the small room. Alex reaches down to shut off the proximity alarm so that the rapid beeping stops. He's about her height, slender of build and with delicate features. That teenaged face, so heartbreakingly beautiful, vulnerable, and young, reminds her of her son. A wave of tenderness surfaces in her before she becomes aware of it and dams it away. She realizes suddenly how little she knows about him, despite chasing after him all these weeks and then capturing him. From time to time, she's seen him tending to the plants in the herbal garden—a small luxury that she allowed herself—with care though she has never told him to do it. Other than that, he's been holed up in his room.

Like with all her prey, she's been avoiding having much interaction with him.

He's cargo, she reminds herself, *worth a lot of money.* A bounty hunter who forgets her job doesn't last very long.

"I'll leave you to it," she says, and starts to move around him to get to the door.

"Wait!" he says. The smirk is gone, replaced by a hesitant, shy smile. "I wanted to tell you that I appreciate your giving me the run of the ship instead of locking me up in a windowless cell or drugging me." He pauses, and then adds, "Also, thanks for not roughing me up."

She shrugs. "Your father's orders were very clear. You're not to be injured or harmed in any way. Not even a scratch on your skin."

"My father." His face becomes expressionless, like a mask. "He told you not to injure me, did he? Well, of course he would."

Alex gives him a thoughtful, but hard, gaze. "But if I feel you're endangering my life, don't you think for a moment I wouldn't put you down."

Ryder lifts his hands in a placating gesture. "I've been good. I promise."

"Honestly, you're not much of a fighter. Besides, it's not like there's anywhere for you to go while we're in hyperspace. Why not let you stretch your legs around the ship?"

"You're not curious about why I ran away and why my father has gone to so much trouble to catch me?"

"I'm paid to get you back to him in one piece," Alex says, "not to ask questions. In my profession, being curious is not always a virtue." *Also,* she adds to herself, *families are impossible for outsiders to understand.*

The smirk is back on his face. He points to the terminal that Alex was using. "You were curious about *that.*"

"I told you, a security precaution."

"You would have found out that it's nothing dangerous within a few seconds. But you played for a while."

"I got pulled in," she says. "It's a game, and on this little ship, I get as bored as you."

He laughs. "So, what do you think?"

She considers the question and decides there's nothing wrong with giving him her honest opinion. A privileged kid like that probably never hears any real criticism. "The set up is good, but the pacing is off. The language is self-indulgent in places, and the Pinocchio storyline is a bit clichéd. Still, I think it has potential."

He nods, acknowledging her feedback. "This is my first time telling a story in this way. Maybe I've added too much."

"You came up with it yourself?"

"In a manner of speaking. You're right that it's not completely original."

"I'd like to play more of it," she says, surprising even herself.

"Go ahead, and keep on telling me what works and what doesn't work."

```
> enter King's bedroom
```

The King's Bedroom
```
The King's bedroom is large, cavernous even. The
Grand Hall is for banquets and stately recep-
tions, but here's where he conducts real busi-
ness and gives the orders that will change the
course of history. (Insofar as issuing an edict
announcing a new tax credit for woodcarvers and
novel spell-casting research can be deemed to
be changing history.)
```

In the middle of the room is a large bed—well, might as well call it king-sized. Around the room are many cabinets filled with many more drawers, all unlabeled, all alike. There's also a writing desk next to the window. The window is very wide and very open, contrary to proper secure palace design principles. But as a result, the room is flooded with light.

Usually this room is filled with people: ministers, guards, generals just back from the front seeking an audience with the King. You've never been here alone before.

Spring clangs in after you.

"We're going to look for the Augustine Module," you say. "That ought to cheer you up, right?"

Spring says nothing.

> examine cabinets

They all look the same. The rows of drawers lining them look, if possible, even more alike. You're not sure which one to start with.

> pick one at random

I only understand you want to pick something.

> open drawer

Which drawer do you mean?

> open all drawers

There are too many drawers to pick from.

"Ryder, I used to play a lot of old games like this. Your puzzles really need some work."
    "You want a hint?"

"Of course not. What would be the point? Might as well have you tell me the story yourself."

"All right."

Alex looks at Ryder. *This is a boy who probably doesn't like to get his hands dirty. He would be used to the many servants and droids back in his father's house. Like a princess.*

```
> go to nearest drawer and open it

If you're thinking of opening every drawer one by
one, the King will be back before you're done.

> Damn it, this is terrible programming!

Spring shifts from one foot to the other behind
you.

"Did you say something about programming?"

> ask Spring about programming

"Since I'm a non-Cartesian automaton, you can
control my behavior with programs." Spring's
voice is dreary and grinds on your ears.

You step up to Spring and open up his front
panel, revealing the spinning gears and rocking
levers within, as well as reams of densely-
punched instructional tape.

(As a shortcut, you may engage in programming
in pseudocode and we'll pretend that they're
translated into the right patterns of holes on
tape—otherwise we'd be here forever.)

> TELL Spring the following:
 >>    WHILE (any drawer is not open)
 >>        PICK a closed drawer at random
 >>        OPEN the drawer
 >>        TAKE OUT everything
 >>    END WHILE
 >>END TELL
```

Spring springs to life and rushes around the room, opening random drawers and dumping the contents on the ground. The floor shakes as his bulk thumps back and forth. Eventually he finishes opening every drawer in the room and stops.

"Your father is not going to be happy about this," he says.

> examine room

There are too many things scattered all over the floor to list them one by one. In fact, you can't even see the floor.

> TELL Spring to sort objects in room by type

Spring whips around the room, sorting objects into neat piles: there's a pile of books, a pile of jewels, a pile of secret files, a pile of parchments, a pile of clothes, a pile of shoes, a pile of nuts (why not? They make good snacks).

"Thanks," you say.

"No problem," Spring says. "Automata are good for this kind of thing."

> TELL Spring to look for Augustine Module

"See, now you're just being lazy," Spring says. "I have no idea what an Augustine Module looks like."

"Very clever," Alex says.
    "Which part?" Ryder looks pleased.
    "Your game lures the player into relying on doing everything by ordering a non-player character around. I suppose this is supposed to get the player to feel a sense of participation in the plight of the oppressed automata in your world? Inducing empathy and guilt is the hardest thing to get right in a game."

Ryder laughs. "Thanks. Maybe you're giving me too much credit. I was just trying to make the time pass somehow. Sometimes the inevitable end doesn't seem so scary if you can keep the silence at bay with a story."

"Like that girl with the stories and the Sultan," she says. She almost adds *and death* but catches herself.

Ryder nods. "I told you. It's not a very original idea."

"This isn't some political commentary on your father's opposition to strong AI, is it? You're one of those free-droiders." She's used to her prey telling her stories to try to get her to be on their side, to let them go. Using a game to do it is at least a new tactic.

Ryder looks away. "My father and I didn't discuss politics much."

When he speaks again, his tone is upbeat, and Alex gets the impression he's trying to change the subject. "I'm surprised you caught on so quick. The text-based user interface is primitive, but it's the best I can do given what I have to work with."

"When I was little, my mother allowed only text-based streams on the time-sharing entertainment clusters because she didn't want us to see and covet all the fancy things we couldn't afford to buy." Alex pauses. It's not like her to reveal a lot of private history to one of her prey. Ryder's game has unsettled her for some reason. What's more, Ryder is the son of the most powerful man on Pele, and she resents the possibility that he might pity her childhood in the slums. She hurries on, trying to disguise her discomfort. "Sometimes the best visuals and sims can't touch plain text. How did you learn to write one?"

"It's not as if you allow me access to any advanced systems on your ship," he says, spreading his hands innocently. "Anyway, I always preferred old toys as a kid: wooden blocks, paper craft, programming antique computers. I guess I just like old-fashioned things."

"I'm old-fashioned myself," she says.

"I noticed. You don't have any androids to help you out on the ship. Even the flight systems are barely automated."

"I find droids creepy," she says. "The skin and flesh feel real, warm and inviting. But then you get to the glowing electronics underneath, the composite skeleton, the thudding pump that simulates a heartbeat as it circulates the nutrient fluid that functions like blood."

"Sounds like you had a bad experience with them."

"Let's just say that there was one time I had to kill a lot of androids used as decoys to get to the real deal."

His face takes on an intense look. "You said 'kill' instead of 'deactivate' or something like that. You think they're alive?"

The turn in the conversation is unexpected, and she wonders if he's manipulating her somehow. But she can't see what the angle is. "It's just the word that came to mind. They look alive; they act alive; they feel alive."

"But they're not really alive," he says. "As long as their neural nets do not surpass the PKD-threshold, androids aren't self-aware and can't be deemed conscious."

"Good thing making supra-PKD androids is illegal," she says. "Otherwise people like you would be accusing me of murder."

"How do you know you've never killed one? Just because they're illegal doesn't mean they aren't made."

She considers this for a moment. Then shrugs. "If I can't tell the difference, it doesn't matter. No jury on Pele would convict me anyway for killing an android, supra-PKD or not."

"You sound like my father, all this talk of laws and appearances. Don't you ever think deeper than that?"

Can this be the secret that divided father from son? Youthful contempt for the lack of idealism in the old? "I don't need a lecture from you, and I'm certainly not interested in philosophy. I don't care for androids much; I'm just glad I can get rid of them when I need to. A lot of my targets these days pay for android decoys to throw me off—I'm surprised you didn't."

"That's disgusting," Ryder says. The vehemence in his voice surprises her. It's the most emotional she's ever seen him, even more than when she had caught him hiding in the slums on the dark side of Ranginui—it hadn't been that hard to find him; when the senior senator from Pele wanted someone found, there were resources not otherwise available. When Alex had called out his real name in the crowded hostel, Ryder had looked surprised for a moment, but then quickly appeared resigned, the light in his eyes dimming.

"To make them die for you," he continues, his voice breaking, "to . . . *use* them that way."

"In your case," Alex says dispassionately, "decoys would have helped you out and made my life harder, but I suppose you didn't get to take much money when you ran away from home. You need to spend a lot to get them custom made to look like you. Bad game plan on your part."

"Is your job just a game to you? A thrilling hunt?"

Alex doesn't lose her cool. She's used to histrionics from her prey. "I don't usually defend myself, but I don't usually talk this much with one of my prey either. I live by the bounty hunter's code: whether something feels right or wrong changes depending on who's telling the story, but what doesn't change is that we have a role to play in someone else's story—bringer of justice, villain, minor functionary. We're never the stars of the stories we're in, so it's our job to play that role as well as we can.

"The people I'm paid to catch *are* the stars of their own stories. And they've all chosen to do something that would make my clients want to pay to have them found. They made a decision, and they must live with the consequences. That is all I need to know. They run, and I pursue. It's as fair a fight as life can give you."

When Ryder speaks again, his voice is calm and cool, as if the outburst never happened. "We don't have to talk about this. Let me work on the game some more. Maybe you'll like what happens next better."

They hold each other's gaze for a long moment. Then Alex shrugs and leaves the room.

```
> examine pile of books
```

There are treatises on the History of Chrysanthemum, the Geography of the World, the Habits of Sheep (Including Diseases and Treatment Thereof), and the Practice of Building Clockwork Automata . . .

```
> read History of Chrysanthemum
```

You flip the thin book open to a random page, and begin to read:

> *Thereafter Chrysanthemum became the Hegemon of the Pan-Flores League, holding sway over all the cities of the peninsula. The Electors from all the cities choose a head of the league from the prominent citizens of Chrysanthemum. Though elected, the league head continued to hold the title of King. The election campaigns often kept those who would be King far from home as they curried favor with the Electors in each member city.*

> read Sheep book

From behind you, Spring says, "Why are you reading about sheep instead of figuring out how to help me?"

> read Clockwork Automata

You flip open the heavy book, and the creased spine leads naturally to a page, one apparently often examined.

> *St. Augustine wrote, "It is one thing to be ignorant, and another thing to be un-willing to know. For the will is at fault in the case of the man of whom it is said, 'He is not inclined to understand, so as to do good.'*
> "The Augustine Module is a small jewel that, when inserted into an automaton, endows the automaton with free will. A pulsing, shimmering, rainbow-hued crystal about the size of a walnut, it is found only in the depths of the richest diamond mines. The laws of the realm forbid the production of such automata, for it is only the place of God, not Man, to endow creatures with free will.
> Miners believe that the presence of the Augustine Module may be detected by the use of the HCROT. By the principle of sympathetic vibration, a HCROT is equipped with a crystal that, when heated, will vibrate near the presence of any Augustine Module. The closer the module is to the HCROT, the stronger the vibrations.

> ask Spring about HCROT

Spring shakes his head. "Never heard of it."

> examine pile of jewels

There are rubies, sapphires, pearls, corals, opals, emeralds. Their beauty is dazzling.

Spring speaks up, "I don't think your father would store an Augustine Module here."

"Why not?" you ask.

"Every year, he issues ever more severe edicts against the use of the Augustine Module in the construction of automata. Why would he store any here, where his ministers and generals might find them?"

"You really don't like your father's politics, do you?" asks Alex.

"I told you: we didn't talk about politics much."

"You haven't answered my question. I think it really bugs you that your father advocates against sentience for androids. But you know that Pele is a conservative world. He has to say certain things to get elected." A thought occurs to her. "Maybe your secret is that you know something about him that will destroy his political career, and he doesn't want you to be used by his enemies. What is it? Does he have a droid lover? Maybe one that's supra-PKD?" Now she *is* mildly curious.

Ryder laughs bitterly.

"No, that's too obvious," Alex muses. "It's all in your game. Was there really a toy soldier? A childhood companion you wanted to make fully alive but your father wouldn't budge on? Is that what this is all about?" As she speaks, Alex can feel anger rise in herself. The whole thing seems frivolous, utterly absurd. Ryder was a spoiled rich little kid whose daddy issues amounted to not getting his way about some toy.

"I never got to see my father much," Ryder says. "It seemed that he was always out traveling around Pele, campaigning for re-election. I spent a lot of time at home with androids. I grew up with them."

"So you felt close to them," Alex says. "While you were fretting about 'freedom' for your toys, there were people worried sick about how to feed their children outside your mansion. How can a human compete against an android who's just as creative and resourceful when the human needs rest, might get hurt, might get sick? Your father pushed hard against sentience for androids so that actual people, real people like my parents, would still have jobs."

Ryder does not flinch away from Alex's gaze. "The world is filled with multitudes of suffering, and we are limited by our station in life to focus on what we can. You're right: since the androids aren't sentient, no one thinks there's anything wrong with exploiting them the way we are. But we *can* make them sentient with almost no effort; we've known how to cross the PKD-threshold for decades. We simply *choose* not to. You don't see a problem with that?"

"No."

"My father would agree with you. He would say there's a difference between acts of omission and commission. Withholding from the androids what they could be easily given, unlike taking away what has already been given, does not constitute a moral harm. But I happen to disagree."

"I told you," Alex says, "I'm not interested in philosophy."

"And so we continue to engage in slavery by a philosophical sleight of hand, through deprivation."

The flight computer crackles to life. "Exiting hyperspace in half an hour."

Alex looks at Ryder, her face cold. "Come on, let's go."

They proceed together to the cockpit, where Alex waits for Ryder to lie down in the passenger seat. "Hands on the armrests. I have to secure you," she says.

Ryder looks up at her, his delicate features settling into a look of sorrow. "All these days on the same ship and you still don't trust me?"

"If you're going to make a move, re-entry is the time to do it. I can't take a chance. Sorry." She activates the chair's restraint system and flexible bands shoot out from the chair to wrap themselves around Ryder's shoulders, hips, chest, legs. The bands tighten and Ryder groans. Alex is unmoved.

As Alex reaches the door of the cockpit, Ryder calls after her, "You're really going to turn me over to my father when you don't even know what this is about?"

"I understand enough to know I don't care about your pet cause."

"I began my life with stories others told me: where I come from, who I am, who I should be. I've simply decided to tell my own story. Is that so wrong?"

"It's not for me to judge the right or wrong of it. I know what I need to know."

"It is one thing to be ignorant, and another thing to be unwilling to know."

She says nothing and leaves the cockpit.

She knows she should get ready for re-entry and check on the flight systems one last time before securing herself in the pilot's chair.

But she turns back to the terminal. There's still a bit of time. She won't admit it to Ryder, but she *does* want to know how the game ends, even if it's probably nothing more than the self-indulgent ravings of a disappointed child.

"But my father must be storing the contraband Augustine Modules he's seized somewhere in the Palace," you say. "The question is where."

"What room have you never been inside of?"

> south

Outside the King's and Queen's Bedrooms
Spring clangs after you.

> TELL Spring to break down the door to Queen's bedroom

"As you wish, Princess."

Spring charges against the door and, amazingly, the door holds for a second. Then it crumbles.

> enter Queen's bedroom

The Queen's Bedroom
You can't remember ever having been inside the Queen's bedroom. The bed, the dressers, and the cabinets are all faded, as if the color has been leached out of them. There's layer of dust over everything, and cobwebs hang from the ceiling and the furniture. The tapestries hanging against the walls have been chewed into filigree by moths.

There's a painting hanging on the wall next to the window. Under the painting is a desk full of cubbyholes stuffed with parchment.

> examine painting

You make your way through the musty room to look
at the painting. The dust motes you've disturbed
twirl though the air, lit only by a few bright
beams coming through cracks in the shutters.

The man in the painting is your father, the King.
He looks very handsome with his crown and ermine
robe. He sits with a young girl on his lap.

"She looks like you," says Spring.

"She does," you say. The girl in the painting
is five or six, but you don't remember sitting
with your father for this portrait.

> examine cubbyholes in desk

You retrieve the sheets of parchment from the
cubbyholes. They look like a stack of letters.

> examine letters

You read aloud from the first letter.

   My Darling,

   I am sorry to hear that you're unwell. But
   I simply cannot leave the campaign to come
   home right now. By all signs, the election
   will be close. Not that I expect you to
   understand, but if I leave here, Cedric
   will be able to convince the Electors of
   Peony that they should throw their support
   behind him.
      *You must listen to the Castellan and not
   give the clockwork servants any trouble.*

   Your ever-loving father.

Spring shuffles behind you.

"Cedric challenged your father four years ago," Spring says.

"I don't remember being sick then," you say. "Or writing to him."

In fact, you don't remember much about the election at all. You remember reading about it and hearing others talk about it. But now that you think about it, you have no personal memories from that time at all.

You don't like the strange feeling in your heart, so you try to change the subject.

"I think we should look for the Augustine Module," you say.

"We'll need a HCROT," says Spring. "Have you figured out what is a HCROT?"

> say "no"

(to Spring)

"Then what are you going to do?"

> wander around the room aimlessly

Oh, that is a good plan.

No, actually I meant that's a terrible plan.

> jump up and down

You're looking silly.

Have we reached the try-anything-once part of the adventure?

> shake fist at Ryder

What are you supposed to do in an adventure whenever you're stuck?

> inventory

You're carrying the following items:

A sheaf of letters

An unlit torch, half filled with oil

> Ha! I got it, Ryder!

I don't understand what you want to do.

> TELL Spring to light torch

Spring takes the torch from you.

He opens up his front panel, revealing the whirling gears inside. He touches the tip of one of his steel fingers against a spinning gear and sparks fly out. One of them lands on the torch. The smell of rose fills the room, dispelling the musty smell.

Spring hands the lit torch to you.

> shake torch

You hear something rattle inside the torch, a crystalline sound.

> hold torch upside down

Some of the oil drip out, but the rest, remarkably, stays put. You can feel the handle of the torch grow hot.

A rattling sound comes from inside the torch, eventually settling into a rapid tap-tap-tap.

"A TORCH," you say triumphantly, "becomes a HCROT when turned around."

Spring claps.

> move left

You are next to the wall.

The torch in your hand emits the same rattle.

> move forward

You move towards the window.

The torch in your hand emits the same rattle.

> move right

You're standing in front of the desk.

The torch in your hand emits the same rattle.

Spring looks at you. "I don't hear any difference."

"I think it's supposed to vibrate faster and make a different sound when it gets closer to the Augustine Module," you say. "Supposed to. Maybe we need something else."

> inventory

You're carrying a sheaf of letters.

> examine letters

You have a burning torch held upside down in your hand. If you try that you're going to burn the letters before you can read them.

> hand torch to Spring

Spring takes the torch from you.

"You might as well move around the room a bit," you say. "Try the corners I haven't tried."

> examine letters

You read aloud from the next letter.

Castellan,

I am utterly devastated at this news.
    Please have the body embalmed but do not bury her yet. Do not release the news until I figure out what to do.

Spring has wandered some distance away. The rattling in the torch has slowed down, more like a tap, tap, tap.

You're too stunned by what you're reading to stop. You turn to the next letter.

Artificer,

I would like you to fashion an automaton that is an exact replica of my poor, darling Alex. It must be so life-like that no one can tell them apart.
    When the automaton is complete, you must install in it the jewel I have enclosed with this letter. Then you may dispose of the body
    No, do not refuse. I know that you know what it is. If you refuse, I shall make it so that you will never create anything again.
    The campaign is so heated here that I cannot step away and let Cedric sway them. Yet, if the news is released that my daughter is dead and I am refusing to go home to mourn her, Cedric will make hay

of it and make me appear to be some kind
of monster.
   No, there is only one solution. No one
must know that Alex has died.

Spring is now in the hallway. The rattling in
the torch has slowed down to an occasional tap,
like the start of a gentle bit of rain. Tap . . .
Tap . . . Tap . . .

> TELL Spring to return

Spring comes closer. Tap, tap, tap.

Spring is now next to you. Tap-tap-tap.

> TELL Spring to hand over the torch

Spring hands the torch to you. Tap-tap-tap.

"Did you know?" you ask.

"I have been with you for only four years,"
Spring says.

"But I remember playing with you when I was a
baby! You never told me they weren't real memories."

Spring shrugs. The sound is harsh, mechanical.
"Your father programmed me. I do what I'm told
to do. I know what I'm told to know."

You think about the letters. You think about
how vague and hazy your memories of your childhood are, how nothing in those memories is ever
distinct, as if they were stories told to you a
hundred times until they seemed real.

You bring the torch closer to your chest. The
heat makes you flinch. TapTapTap.

You wonder where she's buried. Is it in the garden, right underneath your bedroom window, where the lilies bloom? Or is it further back, in the clearing in the woods where you like to catch fireflies at night?

You bring the torch even closer. The flame licks at your hair and a few strands curl and singe. Tttttap.

You tear open the dress on you to reveal the flesh beneath. You put a hand against your chest and feel the pulsing under the skin. You wonder what will happen if you slash it open with a knife.

Will you see a beating heart? Or whirling gears and tightly-wound springs surrounding a rainbow-hued jewel?

It is one thing to be ignorant, and another thing to be unwilling to know.

>

ABOUT THE AUTHOR

Ken Liu is an author and translator of speculative fiction, as well as a lawyer and programmer. His fiction has appeared in *The Magazine of Fantasy & Science Fiction, Asimov's, Analog, Clarkesworld, Lightspeed,* and *Strange Horizons,* among other places. He has won a Nebula, two Hugos, a World Fantasy Award, and a Science Fiction & Fantasy Translation Award, and been nominated for the Sturgeon and the Locus Awards. He lives with his family near Boston, Massachusetts.

Ken's debut novel, *The Chrysanthemum and the Dandelion,* the first in a fantasy series, will be published by Simon & Schuster's new genre fiction imprint in 2015, along with a collection of short stories.

Grave of the Fireflies
CHENG JINGBO, TRANSLATED BY KEN LIU

February 16: Through the Door Into Summer

The Snow-No-More birds appeared in the sky, adding to the chaos that enveloped the world.

The fluttering wings that were supposed to signal clear weather scraped across the orange sky like the return of snow-laden billows. Ash-white feathers filled the air, drifting down until they fell into the black orbs of my eyes, turning them into snowy globes.

On the sixteenth of February, I was born on the road to light, a refugee. My ebony eyes were luminous and vivid, but no one came to kiss my forehead. All around, people sighed heavily. I lifted my head and saw the ash-white flock heading southwards, their cries as dense as their light-stealing wings.

To the south was the Door Into Summer, built from floating asteroids like a road to heaven.

The giant star that lit the way for the refugees gradually dimmed, the shadow crawling up everyone's face. After the briefest experience of daylight, I saw the first twilight of my life: my mother's image bloomed in the dim light like a secret flower.

Mankind streamed across the river of time, aiming straight for the Door Into Summer. In that moment, our tiny planet was falling like a single drop of dew in a boundless universe, tumbling towards that plane made up of the broken remains of a planet.

New cries arose from the Snow-No-More birds. Gliding through the gravity-torn clouds, the soft, gentle creatures were suddenly seized by some unknown force. Alarmed, the flock wound through the sky like a giant electric eel, each individual bird a scale. They hovered near each other, their wingtips brushing from time to time with light snaps. Quickly, the snaps grew louder and denser—the birds drew closer together to resist the unknown force that threatened to divert them, and electric sparks generated by the friction of the wings hopped from wingtip to wingtip. A great, invisible hand wrapped its fingers around the throat of the flock, and the ash-white electric eel in the sky began to tremble, its entire body enshrouded by a blue flame.

And in a moment, the invisible force that had been pulling them higher into the sky dissipated. The eel writhed in its death throes among the clouds, the feathers shed by struggling birds falling like volcanic ash. Soon, the feathery snow descended over us. They slid in through gaps around the oxhide flaps, fell, moth-like, against the greasy glass of the gas lamps, floated in clumps over the dirty water in copper basins, caught in my eyebrows and the corners of my eyes.

The oxcart rolled forward slowly. My mother began to sing in the midst of this snowstorm of ash and sorrow. Gradually, I fell asleep, listening to her lovely voice. But her eyes were filled with the sights from outside the cart: in the suffocating, fiery air, tens of thousands of oxcarts headed in the same direction. The remnants of humanity flooded across the hills and plains. The further she looked, the more oxcarts she saw—each like the one we were in.

An old man rushed before our cart and knelt down. "The star is about to go out."

Even before he had spoken, my mother already knew about the star. Even before he had opened his lips, her eyes had already sunken into gloom. Since the oxen's eyes were covered by black cloth, the animals showed no signs of panic. But as the darkness fell, they felt the strange chill.

Rising clouds of dust drowned out the old man's words, just like the endless night drowned my mother's beautiful, bottomless eyes.

He had failed to notice the spiked wheels of the oxcart. Blood soaked into earth, a dark stain melting into the night. In my sleep, I felt the oxcart lurch momentarily, as though something had caught against its wheels. And then it rolled on as though nothing had happened.

My mother continued to sing. In her song, the white-bearded High Priest died on the way to see the Queen—because the news he was bringing was ill.

After that day, I never saw a Snow-No-More bird again.

Legend has it that on the day I was born, my small planet passed through the Door Into Summer. All the Snow-No-More birds died outside the door. Though they were birds of spring, when they died, it snowed: every flake was an ash-white feather; every flake was limned in pale blue fire.

On the day the Snow-No-More birds disappeared in the southern sky, we penetrated a wall made of 1301 asteroids and exited the Garden of Death through the Door Into Summer.

February 19: Curtain Call for the Crimson Universe

People called me Rosamund because, they said, I'm the rose of the world.

I thought the world was a fading rose. The cooling universe was filled with ancient stars like our sun—they collapsed, lost heat, aged, contracted into infinitesimal versions of themselves and stopped giving us light. Now, with shrunken bodies and failing sights, they could only offer us a useless prayer as they watched us flee at the edge of night.

A thousand years ago, nine priests secretly debated among themselves around a circular table and probed the will of the gods for the answer to the question: why had the stars suddenly decided to grow old and die? In the end, because they could not answer the question satisfactorily, the king punished them by taking their heads.

But one of them, the most powerful priest of them all, managed to survive. He lived because he had two faces, the second one hidden by his long, thick hair, and no one ever knew of its existence. If one gathered enough courage to pull aside the curtain of snake-like hair, one would see tightly pursed lips and wide-open eyes. When the king demanded that the priests yield up their heads, this priest split apart his own head with a double-edged sword and gave up the front half. Thereafter he became a wanderer far from home, and lived only with the secret half of his head.

It was rumored that the descendants of this man created Weightless City, the first planet we arrived at after passing through the Door Into Summer. The star collapsed behind us while the army of refugees dove like moths towards the last lit lamp in the universe.

No one could explain why the stars were dying. A thousand years ago, following an ancient prophecy, our ancestors altered the structure of our planet and adjusted its gravity to turn it into an Ark to flee towards those stars that seemed young still.

When we arrived at Weightless City, everyone was going to leave our own planet and move there. After its thousand-year flight, the Ark could no longer go on. And after we left our home, this planet that had once birthed and nurtured all of humanity would fall into the heat of a strange star and dissolve into a million droplets of dew.

That year, I turned six. The nineteenth of February was a special day. My mother, the Queen, set me on the back of a white bull, and

I saw thousands, tens of thousands of oxen, all of them pitch black, pulling my subjects over the earth like a flood.

A lonely, golden tower rose from the distant horizon. By dusk, the refugees arrived at its foot. The tower, too, appeared as if it had been on a long journey. Behind the tower was a deep trench like a surgical incision; the rich, fleshy loam brought up from its depths gave off a burnt scent.

This was the Dock. The inhabitants of Weightless City, the dark green planet revolving overhead, had dropped it down. On this special day, the gravity between the two planets achieved perfect balance, enabling us to ascend this tower to our new home.

If anyone could have witnessed the coupling between these two tiny planets from a distance, they would have seen this: a golden rod emerged from one of the planets like a raised matchstick. As the two planets spun, the matchstick struck the surface of the other planet, scratching out a groove on its surface, and then stopped.

But for those on the ground, the sight seemed like a manifestation of divinity. Occasionally, through an opening in the clouds, we could see our future home—dark green, serene Weightless City. The mammoth golden tower in front of us had extended from that heaven like a dream, and then fixed itself inexorably into the earth. Everyone cried out in joy. They busied themselves with re-shoeing the oxen with strong, magnetic shoes, gilding the wheel spikes with silvery powder, patching the leaky oxhide tents . . .

Afterwards, the oxcarts began to climb the tower in order of precedence. Far away from the tower, I ran, barefoot. A few flowers hid in the grass, twinkling here and there. Wind seemed to come from somewhere deep within the ground, and I thought I heard a voice cry out between sky and earth: *Rosamund, Rosamund.* I placed my ear against the tips of the blades of grass: I wanted to know if it was my planet calling my name.

When I turned to look back, I saw the sky turn slowly, the horizon already tilted. The tower leaned away from the zenith until, finally, anyone could walk on it barefoot, like me.

Night fell, and the whole human race trod along this road to heaven. A woman carelessly knocked over a kitchen pail, and it fell all the way down the tower, clanging, banging all the way, until it plunged into a black, moist cloud, leaving nothing but ripples on the surface. It was so quiet that everyone heard the woman muttering her complaint. But then she pulled the rope attached to the pail—almost everything in the oxcarts had been tied down by rope to prevent it from moving about during the journey—and so her pail returned, filled with clear water.

We marched in the dark, silent night. In front of us was a new city, shining like a piece of jade. Around the massive and long bridge formed by the golden tower, all we could see was the star-studded night.

The universe was alike a gigantic stage curtain that gradually fell. Fewer and fewer stars remained. We walked faster.

February 22, The Magician of Weightless City

My mother was the only one who did not cry after she saw Weightless City.

After we descended the tower, the sky rotated back into its original location. The horizon was no longer tilted. Everyone got a clear view of heaven: just another ruin.

This was the first thing my mother said to the first stranger she met: "Take me to your king, archon, headman, or . . . whatever you call him."

"There's no one like that here," the man answered. "We just have a magician."

And so we came upon a machine-man made of steel. It sat in the middle of an open space like a heap of twisted metal. Walking from its left foot to its right foot took five minutes. But to climb from its right foot to its waist took a whole afternoon.

"Listen," my mother said. She squatted down to look into my eyes. "Rosamund, my precious, I have to go in there to talk to the magician. Wait for me here. My darling, my baby, do not leave before I come out."

I nodded. She smiled and lightly kissed my forehead. No one saw this farewell, and that was why, in the stories that people told afterwards, the Queen died from mistakenly eating a poisonous mushroom in Weightless City. But I saw with my own eyes my mother climb onto the shoulder of that gigantic robot, enter through an ear, and then disappear.

In the six years after I became an orphan, after my planet and my mother had abandoned and forgotten me, I grew into a twelve-year-old, willful young woman. Everyone now called me Wild Rose.

In the new world of Weightless City, I discovered a plant that had also existed on my planet. The vines extended hundreds of miles, and had fragile stalks that ended in delicate, thin tips. I liked to run among them barefoot. As my feet crushed the stalks, bright yellow liquid oozed out, and the wind brought indistinct cries: *Rosamund, Rosamund*. I put my ear against the black soil: I wanted to know if it was my planet calling me now through this new earth. My loneliness grew without cease during those six years until it took root deep in my blood and bones.

One time, when I heard the calls and put my ear against the muddy earth, I closed my eyes and saw my mother's face. "Rosamund, my precious . . . " She smiled and kissed my forehead, as though I really were the world's rose. Then I opened my eyes. Nothing.

Another time, when I opened my eyes, what I saw shocked and frightened me: a young man (barely more than a boy) was puffing out his cheeks. He was buried in the earth up to his neck, but his face was practically touching my forehead. He blinked his eyes, blue as water, and a breeze caressed my face. I stood up. "Who are you?"

"A free person of Weightless City," he said, joy in his voice. As he answered, he climbed out from his hole nimbly, as though the earth provided no resistance at all. "But who are you?"

I looked at him, stunned. He brushed off the mud from his clothes. There were flowers blooming now in the place where he had been buried.

"Let me guess," he said. "I bet I can guess your name."

And so he found a comfortable place and sat down, and set himself to the serious task of guessing my name.

It was an unforgettable sight: the silhouette of a young man sitting alone in the light of dawn. I couldn't see his face, but I could imagine his expression. Slender grass shot up wildly around him, extending further and further away.

"All right," he said, finally. "I give up. Why don't you try to guess my name?"

But then he glanced up at the sky and slapped his head. "Ah, I forgot what I came for. Rosamund, my sweet girl, where are you?"

As he said this, he was already running away like the wind. And so I had no choice but to cup my hands around my mouth and shout at his back, "Do you know Rosamund?"

"No." He was already some distance away. "I have to find her first. And then I'll know her."

"Why are you looking for Rosamund?"

He was almost at the horizon. "Because she's my guest."

I sighed. He was already invisible. "*I* am Rosamund."

A whirlwind swept from the horizon. The young man was standing in front of me again. He combed his hair with his hands, smoothed out the wrinkles on his shirt, and then bowed towards me very chivalrously. "Pleased to make your acquaintance, my . . . guest."

"But who are you?"

"Neither of us could guess the other's name. If you're truly Rosamund, then permit me to present you with my true name: the Magician of Weightless City."

Six years after meeting me, the Magician of Weightless City no longer looked so young. His castle was the secret to his eternal youth.

But I still enjoyed running barefoot on the wild heath. To see me, he often had to leave his castle. And in this way we grew up together.

Now that I was eighteen, he was like a knight, with a steel will and iron-hard shoulders. But when I was twelve, I had entered his castle for the first time.

The castle was the silent robot sitting on the ground. Since the robot had no need of a bladder, that was the location of the castle gate. After we entered, the Magician (still boyish back then) held my hand with his right hand, and with a *puff*, a torch appeared in his left hand. The interior of the castle was completely dark.

We passed by many murals, set foot on countless carpets, and after the seventh turn in the staircase, we knocked over three silver bottles and a crystal ball. His eyes and hair glinted brightly in the light from the torch. Both of us talked only of the journey we had taken and what we had encountered along the way, as though we hadn't been paying attention to each other at all.

Finally, I saw my mother, sitting on a chair covered by a tiger skin. She looked serene; her face hadn't changed at all from how I remembered her.

"Let me take a look at you, young lady," she said. Then she recognized me with a start. "What in the world happened to you?"

The Magician clapped his hands, and the torch disappeared from his left hand. Innumerable points of light suddenly appeared in the dark ceiling of the great hall, like stars, like fireflies.

The man who brought forth light said to my mother, "Your Majesty, while you have only been here a little while, she has been living outside on her own for six years."

"What kind of witchcraft is this?!" She hugged me and then pushed me back, holding onto my arms tightly so that she could examine me in detail. I was too embarrassed to look back at her.

The Magician said, "A thousand years ago, one of my ancestors came through the Door Into Summer. Using magic and witchcraft, he built this castle of eternal youth. Whether something is living or dead, as soon as it comes inside, it ceases to be eroded by the river of time. The short periods that I have lived outside the castle caused me to grow into this boyish form you see."

My mother spoke in the darkness. The starry light that bathed her forehead could not illuminate her eyes. The Queen confirmed the claim of this fugitive's descendant to his domain and made him Weightless City's first knight.

The answer to this grant of peerless honor came six years later. My knight found the dust-covered silver armor from the depths of the castle, put it on, and bowed slightly to the Queen on her tiger-skin throne. "Please allow me to be Rosamund's knight. She's come of age and ready to have a knight of her own."

I hid in a dark corner, watching him with my wide-open eyes like a fawn.

"Why?" my mother asked.

"Because she needs a knight. Not just any knight, but me. And I need to become the knight for a pure lady. Not just any lady, but her."

"Then," my mother said, "what can a knight do for a princess? Perhaps he doesn't even know what she truly needs, and neither does she."

The Magician of Weightless City, once a proud youth, and now a knight standing tall, full of courage, trembled as he heard this. His cold, rigid shadow stretched long and narrow, and as he trembled, it seemed about to take off from the ground.

Finally, the corners of his mouth lifted, and he answered the woman sitting high on her throne: "The loneliness in her heart is as dark as her eyes. But I will give her eternal light."

And with that, my knight departed his gloomy castle without looking back.

Behind him, the Queen, driven mad by the terror of eternity, screamed, "The stars are going out! You cannot bring back lasting light!"

The stars are going out. You cannot bring back lasting light. But the barefoot princess remained hidden in the darkness, expectant.

February 28: A Skeleton, or Two

I was sick.

I'd lost count of the passing years. Six years? Sixty? Or even six hundred? February 28th was the last day of that suspended period, the end coming like a cliff cleaving space into two halves.

The Queen of mankind had gone mad in the castle. She could not tolerate the erosion of the river of time, and could tolerate even less the passing days that now skipped over her like migrating birds over a forgotten tree. And so she constantly paced the halls of the castle, too frightened to abandon this heaven of eternal life, and yet unable to derive joy from the absolute stillness.

In her face, I could no longer detect the bloom of that secret flower. The permanent starry night of the great hall's ceiling cast two gloomy shadows under her eyes against her pale mask of a face. My mother's once-luminous black eyes, after many, many, *many* years of unchanging life, finally dimmed and merged into the darkness.

I thought of the man who had once built this castle, that great priest with only half of a head. Where had he gone?

When the world outside was drenched in heavy rain, I made torches out of bundles of straw and played hide-and-go-seek in the castle. I passed through room after room, full of dust, perusing books whose pages shattered at my touch—perhaps time had touched them now and then, after all? Among them was a diary, kept by another princess who had lived here long ago. She had poured out her heart through her quill.

Sometimes, I carried an oil lamp, and as its shifting light cast shadows on the walls, they coalesced into unfamiliar faces; sometimes, I lit a candle inside a rose-colored paper lantern, and the light flickered, almost going out.

I walked through the Cimmerian castle, got lost, searched, and occasionally, at the end of a long hallway, I'd see a figure, hear a low murmur, and then everything would once again disappear into darkness and silence—it was my mother, walking, losing her way, seeking, like me.

Finally, our paths brought each of us to the same room, a room I had never been before. Everything inside seemed as new as the long-ago day when the castle had been first erected. I found my mother sitting on the bed, inside the calla-lily-colored netting, sobbing like a ghost. That luxurious room had floor-length curtains, bright red, fresh, as though drops of blood were about to ooze out.

I went up and pulled the bed nets aside. But only a pair of empty sockets greeted me. It was a corpse. He had died long ago.

My game was over. The riddle revealed its answer. This dry husk of a body had once been famous—he was that priest who had escaped, the creator of Weightless City, the powerful wizard who once possessed two faces. I saw a ring on a string around his neck, and when I recognized it, I gasped.

From the day I was born, I also wore such a ring around my neck.

The inside of the ring was etched with a secret: the name of the lover my mother had lost a thousand years ago. He was once the most respected priest in the whole kingdom, but he had fallen in love with the princess, and they made love in her bedroom. The king, furious, ordered his guards to seize all nine high priests and cut off their heads. As for the princess who had lost her virginity, he sealed her inside a bronze mirror—she had been intended for the prince of another kingdom, and was supposed to become a queen beloved by her subjects and husband alike.

I had read this story in an old book, but I did not know that the legendary princess who had been sealed away was, in fact, my mother. The priest with two faces did not have a chance to say goodbye to his beloved. He cut off half of his head, handed it to the king's guards, and then became a fugitive through the Door Into Summer. A thousand years later, the princess awoke from the bronze mirror and became the wife of a king, and then the queen regnant of a people. By the time I was born, my father—who had never gotten my mother's heart—had already disappeared. My mother ruled over her realm as the disaster of the collapsing star unfolded, and then she led her people onto the route that her lover had taken a thousand years earlier.

Though the priest had built this timeless castle to wait for her, she had still come too late.

In his diary, she read of the suffering he had endured for a thousand years. His quill had turned into her lips, and she spoke to him every day. The diary I found had in fact been composed by the priest as he sank into these hallucinated conversations with my mother.

Finally, one day, seized by the ecstasy and rage of waiting, he cut his own heart open. Loneliness poured out of it, bright, fresh, and so he died in this murky castle.

He spent a thousand years to extinguish each and every star; she spent a thousand years to escape to the last star that remained lit. He knew she would come; she knew he would wait—even though when he had cut off half of his head with his sword, he had no chance to tell her anything.

My mother had known the truth for a long time. She had seen in the corpse's empty sockets the cruelest ending possible. From then on, she became an insubstantial ghost wandering through this empty, massive, ancient castle. The fleeting glimpses and murmurs I had caught of her had been nothing but figments of my imagination.

I finally understood why my mother would rather turn her rotting passion into ghosts that danced at the edge of light than set foot outside this eternal hell. When she saw the stars wink out, one after another, she was the happiest woman in the world. When darkness covered her eyes like a flood, she and the man she loved disappeared together on the shore of life and time.

Now that I understood this most impossible love in the world, I found myself an orphan. Truly, this time, my mother and my planet abandoned me.

I lay on the cold floor of the castle, inches and seconds to death.

I seemed to be back on my little planet spinning in space, blue like water. Slender grass shot up wildly around me, extending further and further away. I put my ear to the tips of the grass, a few flowers twinkling here and there. I knew I was going to die. Everyone who was about to die saw visions of the most beautiful scenes she had seen in her life.

I saw all the flowers blooming, the rain falling, a bright red lantern shining in the forest. I saw legends that flared up and dimmed, the face of a youth, fragile but stubborn grass. I saw the Magician of Weightless City: his silver armor had been burnished by the ice and snow at the peak of the world's tallest mountain, had been washed by the water in the deepest ocean, had protected him through desert, swamp, the ruins of mankind's cities and the Eden of fierce beasts, had been borne up a tower that reached into the sky and, following the planet that had abandoned me, reached an undying star—finally, the armor was dented, broken, full of holes. I saw the Magician's long, narrow shadow sweep across the cold floor before my eyes. I saw the return of the Knight of the Rose.

I could recognize only his eyes, the rest of him hidden behind his long-suffering armor. I couldn't tell if his chestnut hair had turned white. I could only smell wind and earth from the wounds in that silver shell.

My knight came before me, opened his left hand: a black pearl.

He found a slender thread and began to pull on it. The black pearl spun in his hand—ah, it was a tiny ball of thread. He pulled and pulled. In this castle of eternal night, the thread seemed to also have no end.

Finally, he picked me up from the floor. Until that moment, his silence had caused me, in my weakened state, to suspect that I had also turned into an insubstantial shade like my mother, a second living ghost wandering through the castle.

He pressed his left hand into my palm and squeezed my fingers into a fist. Then he pulled the rest of the thread out from between my fingers with his right hand. In that moment, I understood that I was still alive.

Thousands, millions of rays of searing light shot out of my clenched fist. He gave me the most dazzling light in the universe, a fistful of fireflies.

The Magician of Weightless City really did bring back a fragment of the star for me. My eyes had never seen such splendor. I saw my birth and death, feathers drifting down like volcanic ash, the clear, distant cries of Snow-No-More birds—that snowstorm had been kept on the other side of the Door Into Summer, and now, the flakes fell into my eyes, dark as night.

My knight bent to kiss my forehead. The luminous heat dissolved his armor. He and I were pierced by a thousand, a million rays.

The light melted our hair and eyes, skin and organs, until he had no more lips, and I had no more forehead. Our bodies were fixed in place: two skeletons with our arms entwined about each other.

Many years later, more explorers would come here. They would smash through the gate in the robot, where the bladder ought to be. They'd walk into the castle and discover in this perpetual radiance a strange skeleton.

"Maybe this was the priest who had escaped tens of thousands of years ago," one of them would say.

The others, after long debate, would reach consensus and publicize the cause for the extinguishing stars: "Due to the irresistible gravity of their mass, red giants tragically collapsed to death after exhausting the fuel in their cores."

They would not be able to search through the entire castle—that fragment of an eternal star would blind many of the explorers. They would not be able to examine that strange skeleton closely because no one dared to look at it directly for even a thousandth of a second.

The priest extinguished all the lanterns in the universe just so that he could recognize the woman he loved at a glance in the flood of refugees. My knight brought back that star fragment so that the inextinguishable flame could warm the loneliness in my dark eyes. The night completed my mother; the day completed me.

Here, in our luminous crypt, the fire can never be blown out.

First published in *Science Fiction: Literary,* July 2005.
First English language publication.

ABOUT THE AUTHOR

Born in 1983, **Cheng Jingbo** is a prominent member of China's new generation of speculative fiction writers. In 2002, Ms. Cheng's story, "Western Paradise," was nominated for the most prestigious SFF award in China—the Galaxy Award. In 2010, her fantasy story, "Lost in Yoyang," won the Special Award for Youth Literature and the Best Short Story Award in the First Nebula Awards for Global Chinese Language Science Fiction. She lives in Chengdu, China, with a cute west highland white terrier and works as a children's book editor.

Wine

YOON HA LEE

The first attack came by starfall, by deathrise. Fire swept out of the darkness, past the great violet curve of the world of Nasteng, like coins from hell's treasuries. Worse than the fire was the metal: creatures of variable form and singing cilia, joining together into colonial masses that floated high above the moon's surface and dripped synthetic insects that ate geometer's traps into its substance.

For decades Nasteng had escaped the notice of the galaxy's wider culture. This was as its Council of Five preferred. They had a secret that other human civilizations would covet. So they hid behind masks of coral and dangling tassels and quantum jewels, and admitted only traders from the most discreet mercantile societies. Now, their secret had gotten out in spite of their precautions.

Nasteng's city-domes were ruptured. The gardens with their flower-chorales of tuned crickets went up in smoke and blood and gouges. Spybirds swooped down with eyes glaring out of their feathers and marked targets for the bomber-drones. People were dragged by the insects into agony-circles, their hair fused together and lit on fire, inelegant torches.

The Council of Five had known that such a day would arrive. For the moment they were safe in their subterranean fastness. But their safety could not last forever. They knew that they could not negotiate with their immediate attackers. The colonial masses did not think in words, did not recognize *negotiation* or *compromise*. They understood only heuristic target recognition and ballistic calculations. If Nasteng had had more technologically advanced defenses, it might have been able to infect the attackers and subvert their programming, but its long isolation and cultural diffidence toward the algorithmic disciplines precluded any such possibility.

One item Nasteng did possess was a beacon. The Falcon Councilor had obtained it generations ago. Her souvenir of that quest was a gash across her cheek that wept tears that dried into crystals hooking into her flesh. At regular intervals she had to rip her face off and allow a new one to grow, or she would have been smothered. You would have thought that she would want as little to do with the beacon as possible. But no: when the Council of Five gathered around a table set with platters of raw meat and the Wine of Blossoms that was their particular privilege, the Falcon Councilor insisted on being the one to activate the beacon.

The beacon was no larger than a child's fist, and was shaped like a ball. Light sheened across it as though it had swallowed furnaces. If you held it to your ear, you could hear a distant music, as of broken glass and glockenspiels hung upside-down and sixteenth notes played upon the spokes of decrepit bicycle wheels.

The Falcon Councilor lifted the beacon, then turned it over. It clung to her palm, pulsing like an unhealthy nacrescence.

"I don't see any point in delay," the Snowcat Councilor said. It wasn't so much that he was always impatient, although he was, as that he had never gotten along with her.

"We have to be sure of what we're doing," the Falcon Councilor said. "There's no way to rescind the signal once sent."

"Falcon," the Tree Councilor said in their voice like shifting rock and gravel. "We wouldn't be here if we weren't sure. Surely you don't think it would be better to die without attempting anything?"

"No, of course not," the Falcon Councilor said.

"Then do whatever it is that you do with that thing," the Snake Councilor said from the dark corner where she was flipping through a book. The book's pages were empty, although some of them had been dog-eared.

The last councilor, the Dragon Councilor, said nothing, only watched with eyes like etched metal. But then, he never spoke, although sometimes he condescended to vote. They were never tempted to disregard him, however. He was, after all, the head of the Gardeners.

"All right," the Falcon Councilor said. She flung the beacon toward the floor. It sheared through the air with a whistle almost too high-pitched to be heard and shattered against the floor.

The beacon's shards could be counted, yet they hurt the eye. They were more like collections of brittle dust than splinters or solids. As the councilors watched, the shards reassembled themselves. Where there had been a single sphere, there were now two. Then both spheres dissipated in a vapor that smelled of antifreeze and disintegrating circuit boards.

"I hope that's not toxic," the Snowcat Councilor said, narrowing his eyes at the Falcon Councilor.

Whatever response she might have thrown back at him was interrupted by the formation of two doors right above the beacon—beacons?—in a jigsaw of fissures.

"Well," the Snake Councilor said softly, "I hope we have enough wine to offer our guests. Assuming they imbibe." The others ignored her, on the chance that she wasn't joking.

Their guests numbered two. They didn't so much step through the doors as emerge like cutouts suddenly fleshed.

The first was a woman, tall, with the finest of veils over her face. She wore soft robes with bruise-colored shadows, and her cloak was edged with dark feathers. The Snake Councilor glanced at the Falcon Councilor, but the latter's face was an unreadable labyrinth of refractions. The other guest was a man, neatly shaven. His hair was black, his eyes of indeterminate color.

The Falcon Councilor inclined her head to them. "We are grateful for your promptness," she said. "We are Nasteng's Council of Five, and the nature of our emergency should be clear to you."

"Yes," the woman said. The man bowed, but did not speak. There was something forced about the curve of his mouth, as though the lips had been sutured together. "You may call me Ahrep-na. I have a great deal of experience with situations like yours. I assume you're familiar with my past successes, but if you need—"

"We know," the Falcon Councilor said. She had heard the name of Ahrep-na, although it was not safe to use it until she had given you permission. It was why she had left Nasteng all those years ago, in search of Ahrep-na's token.

"In that case," Ahrep-na said, "we will need to discuss the contract. My methods are particular."

The Falcon Councilor thought wryly of Nasteng's high generals, some of whom were rather more useful than others. Most of whom were rather less. One of the dangers of having its officers drawn almost exclusively from the nobility, or from people who bought their commissions. "That won't be an issue," she said. Behind her, she heard a harrumph from the Snowcat Councilor, but he didn't interrupt otherwise.

They spoke some more about operational and logistical details, about courtesies blunt and banal, and circled eventually to the matter of payment. Given Ahrep-na's bluntness about everything else, her diffidence about this matter puzzled the Falcon Councilor. But bring it up she did. "Our contracts are tailored to the individual situation," Ahrep-na said. "Up-front, we require—" She named a sum. It was staggering, but so was annihilation.

Finance was not the Falcon Councilor's domain. The Snake Councilor turned to a page in her empty book, frowned at a column of figures that wasn't there, and said, "It will be done in two days."

Ahrep-na's smile was pleased. "We will also require the fruits of a year's harvest."

"You'll have to be more specific," the Falcon Councilor said, as though this were a tedious back-and-forth about supply depots and ammunition.

Ahrep-na wasn't fooled. "This point is nonnegotiable." She offered no elaboration.

The Falcon Councilor opened her mouth. Prompted by some nuance of sound behind her, however, she turned without saying what had come to her mind. *Harvest.* The councilors' secret that was no secret to the outside world anymore: the wine that kept them young.

The other four councilors faced her, united. She had just been outvoted: irregular, but she had no illusions about what they had done behind her back.

"Falcon," the Tree Councilor said, in their unmovable voice, "we are short of options. Our people burn in the streets. Without them, we too will fall. Accept their offer. We knew we were not negotiating from a position of strength."

"We'll regret this," she said bitterly.

"Anything can be survived," the Snowcat Councilor said, "so long as one is still alive to survive it. You're the second-oldest of us. Are you going to fold up and die so easily? Especially since you're the one who brought us the beacon in the first place?"

"It was that or have no last resort at all," she shot back. "Or did you think we would stand a chance against people slavering after the wine?" She looked over her shoulder at Ahrep-na. "Let me ask this, then, Ahrep-na. Are you going to take the Wine of Blossoms for yourself?"

"That is the one of the two guarantees I will offer you," Ahrep-na said easily. "I will not touch your supply of the wine, nor will the soldiers I will raise for you. Or did you think I was human enough to have any use for it?"

The Falcon Councilor was accustomed to envy, or submission, or greed. It had been a long time since she had seen contempt.

"You said two guarantees," she said. "What is the other?"

Ahrep-na's eyes were sweet with malice. The nameless man stared straight ahead. "I will win this for you," Ahrep-na said, "with the mercenaries I raise."

"Of course you will," the Falcon Councilor said, wondering what the trap was. "Very well. We will contract you under those terms."

Ahrep-na's smile was like a honed knife.

His name was Loi Ruharn, and he was one of the councilors' generals. Most people knew him, however, as the Falcon's Whore.

He had been born Korhosh Ruharn, in one of the poorest quarters of the impoverished city-dome known ironically as the Jewel of Nasteng. As a girlform child, Ruharn had played with toys scavenged from stinking trash heaps in alleys, and watched with pinched eyes while his parents argued over which of the religious offerings they had to neglect this month because otherwise they would be too hungry to work, and swore he would never grow up to live in a crowded home with six brothers and sisters, wondering every night if he would be sold to the Gardeners like the daughter of the Ohn family next door.

As soon as he was old enough and strong enough, Ruharn ran away and enlisted in a noble household's private army. He might have died there. While the Council of Five ruled Nasteng entire, they didn't interfere with the nobles' squabbles so long as they didn't threaten the councilors themselves. But Ruharn acquitted himself well in battle, mostly through a combination of suicidal determination and a knack for small-unit tactics, and he rose quickly in the ranks.

That by itself wouldn't have made him remarkable. There were plenty of talented soldiers, and most of them died young anyway, the way battle luck went. Rather, he came to the Falcon Councilor's attention as a minor novelty, as a womanform soldier who lived as a man. For all her years, she'd never taken such a lover before.

The Falcon Councilor wouldn't stoop to take a common-born lover, but that was easy enough to finesse. She offered riches; she offered to buy Ruharn a commission in the Council's own army, and an adoption into a noble family; and most of all she offered a place in her bed. Ruharn wasn't sentimental about the honor of his chosen profession, although he knew what people would be saying about him. He accepted.

Today, almost six months since the invasion had begun, he was pacing in the command bower of the councilors' fastness. It was decorated with vines from which cloudflowers grew. The vines watered themselves, a neat trick. Irritatingly, they also left puddles, which you'd think he'd know to step around by now. The last time he'd yanked off a table runner and used it to soak up the moisture, he'd been yelled at by General Iyuden, who was insufferable about ornamental items. But Iyuden came from one of Nasteng's oldest, wealthiest families. He wasn't about to have that argument with her.

Arrayed before Ruharn were videoscreens of Nasteng's defenses. It didn't take any kind of experience to see how inadequate they had been. He had read the reports and made his recommendations. It wasn't so much that the senior generals had disagreed as that no recommendation would have made much of a difference.

He didn't know what had happened in the four days since the gateway fastness of Istefnis, on the surface, had been crushed into crumbs of marble and metal and human motes by the invaders. But the mercenaries the councilors had hired had brought with them a fleet of starflyers, a horde of groundswarmers. Nasteng's unnamed enemies had slowly fallen back before the onslaught of hellspikes and icemetal bursts and frenzied gnawers. You could, if you were sufficiently innocent of electromagnetic signatures and spectral flourishes, take it for a particularly disorganized fireworks display. Nasteng itself was now haloed by a staggering murdercloud of debris, whether glowing, glimmering, or gyring dark. It was just as well they weren't putting satellites into orbit anytime soon.

Two things bothered Ruharn about the mercenaries' forces, for all their successes. (More than two. But he had to start somewhere.) First was the question of logistics. The senior general had let drop that the contract had mentioned logistical arrangements. As a staff general, Ruharn had hoped to learn details. Had looked, in fact. So far as he could tell, however, the starflyers and groundswarmers had appeared out of nowhere. It wasn't inconceivable that this was advanced foreign technology—there seemed to be a lot of that going around—but it still made him suspicious.

The other thing was the way the mercenaries fought. When the Falcon Councilor had told him about the arrangement—the private conversation, not the staff meeting where he'd heard the official version—she had indicated every faith in the mercenaries' abilities. So far, Ruharn observed that the mercenaries relied on sheer numbers, wave after wave of suffocation rather than strategy. To be sure, the method was *working*, yet he couldn't help feeling the councilors could have spent their coin more wisely.

The councilors' personal army was used primarily for quashing the nobles' personal armies and secondarily for quashing the occasional revolution. So he didn't have great confidence in his conclusions. Yet it was impossible to serve with any diligence without picking up a few fundamentals of the military art.

As it turned out, he was turning the problem over in his mind—it wasn't as if he had a hell of a lot else to do, since for the first time in his so-called career he was caught up on paperwork—when a message made him forget it completely. He found it on top of his correspondence for the afternoon, smuggled in by who knew what method, a note on the back of a flyer. It said, simply, *I need your help.*

Ruharn would have dismissed it as a prank or a trap, except he recognized the handwriting, even twenty-three years later, for all the changes. The writer still had that particular way of drawing crossbars, of slanting hooks. He assumed she still lived in the same house, or at least the same neighborhood, or she would have said something more to guide him.

It wasn't difficult to slip out of the fastness and to the surface, in one of the bubblecars whose use was reserved to the councilors' favorites. The old neighborhood was some six hours away, to the north and east of Istefnis. Ruharn expected to be discovered eventually, but as long as he wasn't caught cheating on the Falcon Councilor, he didn't think there would be any lasting consequences. Assuming he didn't lose his life to some mine while walking down the street, or break his neck tripping over rubble.

The bubblecar's driver was a prim woman in the Falcon Councilor's livery. When she glanced back at Ruharn, her eyes were momentarily sly. Ruharn didn't notice.

During the ride, he alternated between looking out the window and looking at the status displays, which were connected to the moon's defense systems. He wore the plainest clothes he owned, which weren't very, a severe coat over a suit of soft dark brown with gold-embroidered gingko leaves, neatly fitted trousers, and boots likewise embellished with gold. In the neighborhood where he had grown up, the boots alone would have gotten him robbed, which was why he came armed. Two guns and a knife, the latter being ceremonial, but he kept it sharp on principle. Given his childhood, he was actually better in a knife fight than with handguns.

In the neighborhood where he had grown up, you would also have had one hell of a time finding a fence capable of dealing with items so fine, but that didn't mean no one was stupid enough to try. Maybe his uniform would have been a better idea, except he didn't want to give anyone the notion that he was there on official business.

He hadn't been back in twenty-three years, since he had run away, although from time to time he sent money home. No one from his family had ever acknowledged the payments. He hadn't expected them to; would, in fact, have been obscurely humiliated to hear from them.

The bubblecar wound through streets choked by devastation. Devastation was not new to Ruharn. He had grown up with decaying walls and the debris of blown-away hopes. Nor was he a stranger to battlefield ruin: red dried to blots brown-black, lungs sloughed into gray slime, stinging dust in the air. Even so, dry as his eyes were, the pitted streets and pitiful crumpled corpses were somehow different when they were dead at strangers' hands.

"Here we are," the driver said. She didn't bother to hide her skepticism.

"Thank you," Ruharn said distantly. He put on a filter, then stepped out. The bubblecar didn't wait to accelerate away. Sensible woman.

His memory was still good, despite the damage that had been done. Undoubtedly some of it had been local warfare, not recent either. He made his way through the streets, not too fast and not too slow, pricklingly aware that the few survivors were watching him.

The house had changed a little. Ruharn was certain that the old wind chimes had been decorated by little clay flowers. The new ones had what might charitably be described as rotund four-legged animals (what kind was impossible to say). He couldn't, however, discount the possibility that it was the same set of chimes with different decorations. The girl he had known had always liked chimes. He stepped up to the door—if this was an ambush, so be it—and knocked. "Merenne," he called out. "I'm here. It's Ruharn."

For long moments he thought that the house was chewed up and empty inside, that he'd wasted the trip. Then a voice barely familiar, scratchy with hardship, called back, "I'm coming." Soon enough the door opened.

"Merenne," Ruharn said again, voice unsteady. He did not bow. She would have taken offense.

Merenne was shorter than he was, and her hair had gone gray. She looked fifteen years older than he was. In fact she was his younger by six. The clothes she wore were neatly stitched, and patched besides. The shirt was livened by embroidery, mostly geometrical motifs. Ruharn remembered how assiduously they had both picked apart old handkerchiefs and wrapping cloths to scavenge brightly colored thread for the purpose. She had smiled easily then, as a girl, despite the fact that her shoulders were already growing hunched with the work she had to do. He doubted she smiled easily now. She had been his favorite sister, for whom he had saved pittances to trade for candies, whom he had soothed to sleep with bloodthirsty stories (even then he had had an interest in weapons), and he had left her behind without so much as saying goodbye because staying was unbearable.

48

"I didn't think you'd come," she said, as simple and sharp as a mirror-break. And: "I thought something of your old voice would remain. But I wouldn't have known it was you at all. Come in."

Ruharn's mouth twisted. He hadn't thought about his voice, now a tenor, for years. But he stepped through the threshold. The place was too quiet. Where was everyone? Not that he had so much as known that Merenne herself was still alive. For all he knew, some plague had killed them all years ago.

"I almost didn't come," he said. "But I did. Say what you have to say."

Merenne didn't respond, but instead led him through the house. It didn't take long. The Falcon Councilor would have considered it barely adequate as a closet. Ruharn had always been amused by her misconceptions about how many people you could squeeze into shelter if you really had to.

There were three rooms, and people would all have slept together in the largest, partly for warmth, partly for community. The first thing that caught Ruharn's eye was the dolls: two of them, one-third scale. They had been covered neatly by cloths. He wondered if some absent child had left them that way, tucking them in for the night.

The dolls he had grown up playing with had had brass tacks for eyes that were forever falling out. ("Poison gas rots out their eyes in battle," he had said to wide-eyed little Merenne, long ago. It had been funnier then.) The dolls here were made of some smooth, lambent resin, and their eyes shone like sea-lenses over delicately sculpted noses and lips painted perfect dusky pink. Their hair had been carefully styled, with miniature enameled clasps holding the strands in place. He had seen less beautiful statuettes in the councilors' homes.

"Go on," Merenne said. "Look." As he bent to lift one of the cloths, she added, "You used to have a grand-nephew and a grand-niece."

Ruharn didn't ask what if they had been her own grandchildren, or those of their siblings. Or what had happened to their siblings, for that matter.

Beneath the cloth the doll was naked, and he thought of the crude paper dresses that he had sometimes pinned together for Merenne, back when she had had dolls of her own, colored with markers he had stolen from a store. The doll was shaped like a preadolescent boy, but at the join of its legs was a mass that resembled spent bullets melted partly into each other.

In the doll's hand was a toy gun. (At least, he hoped it was a toy.) He eased the gun out of the doll's grip. "A credible Zehnjer 52-3," he said without thinking, "other than the fact that they did the cartridge upside-down."

He became aware that Merenne was staring at him. "You'd think," she said, "I had all this time to get used to the idea of you as a soldier."

Well, it was better than the other things she could be calling him. "You didn't call me here to identify this toy," he said.

"No," Merenne said quietly. "I called you here because the children have been disappearing. I woke in the night and they were gone. The dolls were left as you see them."

"Kidnappers?" Ruharn said dubiously. Poor people's children were terrible currency if you weren't a Gardener. He knew how noisy they got, adorable as they could be. To say nothing of the messes, and the fact that you wouldn't get any decent ransom for them.

Her mouth half-lifted in a ghost of the smile he remembered, as though she knew what he was thinking. Then the smile died. "Ru," she said, "I asked around. No one's seen a Gardener since the children started to vanish."

He said, because he needed to know, "Has payment been left for anyone?" Because it wasn't inconceivable, even in the midst of the crisis, that the councilors would upgrade their system of harvest. So to speak.

Everyone knew how much you could expect for a whole child in the desirable age range, in reasonable health. Even now Ruharn knew. The payment had changed over the years, but it was impossible not to remain aware.

For years he had taken the system for granted, the way everyone had. Part of the bargain, horrible as it was, was that the families who sold their children received something in return. Admittedly the dolls weren't *nothing*, but he doubted that you could sell them for the equivalent sums. Even if it wouldn't surprise him if someone had started collecting the ghoulish things; there were always such people in the world.

"As if people would tell me?" Merenne said. "But no. I haven't heard so much as a rumor. And I looked for payment"—she said this without shame—"but I saw nothing, because it was one of the first things I thought of. Maybe it's a stupid thing to care about, when our world might not survive. But I have to know what happened to them. And you're the only person I could think to ask."

"I know where to start," Ruharn said carefully. "I can't guarantee any results, though. Most especially, I doubt I can bring the children back." Understatement, since he did think the councilors were involved, the way they were involved with everything of note. He had few illusions about his ability to influence any of them, least of all the one who had taken him for a lover.

"I didn't expect that," she said. "Just find out what you can. So that we know what to expect." Her mouth trembled for a moment, so briefly that he almost thought he had imagined it.

Ruharn wondered what to say next. Everything seemed inadequate. At last he said, "Sometime after this is over, if I ever see you again, tell me their names." He didn't mention death-offerings. The deaths of children, especially small children, were so unremarkable that few people bothered.

Merenne eyed him thoughtfully. "I'll think about it," she said.

He smiled. He had always liked her honesty. After all, it wasn't as if she owed him anything. "All right," he said. "Let me take one of the dolls."

"Take both," Merenne said, with commendable steadiness. "It's not as if they do me any good."

He gathered them up under one arm. Considered resting his free hand on her shoulder, then decided that he had better not. This time he did bow, although he spun on his heel before he could see the expression that crossed her face, and walked out of the house. She didn't follow him or call out a farewell.

The Falcon Councilor did not greet Ruharn when he returned to the underground fastness. One of the servants did, however, present him a note upon paper-of-petals. It instructed him to attend her that night.

First he took the precaution of wrapping up the dolls and putting them in a case that he bullied out of Supply. The supply officer looked at him oddly, but he gave no explanation. It wasn't as if he owed one.

Ruharn reported next to the generals' bower, and stood at attention in the doorway. General Khy sat at a table with her feet on a chair, playing cards with her aide. She was a woman once handsome, but still dangerous, with hair shaved short and a conspicuous blank expanse where her medals should have been; she declined to wear them even on occasions of state. As one of the senior generals, she had taken Nasteng's impotence hard. She and her cards were always here, and even now, as her aide contemplated options, Khy brought up a map to study the latest intelligence.

A quartet of cards burned for additional points sobbed prettily as they crumpled into ashes. Ruharn wished Khy wouldn't use that particular feature, but Khy was entertained by the oddest things. Besides, she was one of the generals who understood strategy, so he preferred not to pick fights with her, on the grounds that she was more important than he was.

Khy liked Ruharn, a fact that he tried not to think too hard about. She waved her hand at him while assiduously keeping the cards' faces out of her aide's view. "General Loi," she said genially. "At ease."

It took a moment for him to recognize the house name he used now. Funny how long it had been since he'd lapsed. "General," Ruharn said. "Any interesting developments?" He doubted it: Khy would hardly be tormenting her cards if something that required her attention were going on.

She sneered, which took him by surprise because she ordinarily approached everything with cockeyed levity. "Look," she said, and flung her cards down. Her aide kept them from fluttering off the edge of the table.

Khy's hands tapped rapid patterns on the nearest interface. Maps flowered, crisscrossed by troop vectors and dotted by the bright double-squares of bases, the cluster-clouds of aerospace fighters. Nasteng's forces were violet. The enemy was green. The mercenaries were gold. Her hands tapped again. The troops moved as their positions and engagements were replayed over time.

"We might as well retire now," Khy said. "Oh, maybe not you, you're young yet, and there's always a use for good staffers." From anyone else it would have been a veiled insult, but Khy had never treated Ruharn as anything but a competent colleague and Ruharn was not so paranoid as to believe that things were different now. "But look, the mercenaries are doing all the work."

"That doesn't mean there won't be more attacks, now that the outsiders know we're here," Ruharn said. And, when Khy didn't respond, he hesitated, then said: "The mercenaries fight with numbers. But they don't fight *well*."

"You're one of the people who can see it, let alone who is willing to *say* it," Khy said bitterly. She flipped a pointer out of her belt, caught it, switched it on. Scribbled indications, in light and hissing sparks, on the maps. "There, there, there, *there*. Victory by attrition. So *wasteful*."

"I understand there's a noninterference clause," Ruharn said neutrally.

"Noninterference, hell. I've had the scanners on it and they can't even tell what our allies *are*. They come from nowhere and the corpses of their units degenerate with astonishing rapidity. There's probably a paper in it for some scientist somewhere."

Khy brought up more photos and videos. At first Ruharn didn't recognize what he was seeing, too busy being distracted by fractal damage, stress marks, metal sheening red-orange in response to unhealthy radiations. Familiar shapes.

Except those weren't the only familiar shapes. Burnt into the wreckage were symbols he remembered from his childhood. The depressions of board games he had played in the dirt, or score-tallies chalked onto walls, or warding-signs around which he and his friends had danced in circles, chanting rhymes to keep the Gardeners away. He glanced sideways at Khy, wondering, but she met his eyes with no sign that she saw anything in the faint symbols at all.

Then again, Khy would have grown up playing board games with real boards, made of marble or jade or mahogany veneer. If she played in the dirt, it would have been in a high-walled, well-tended garden while watched by anxious servants and the occasional guard. And she would never have had to worry about being sold to the Gardeners.

Still, it was dismaying to have one of the generals he respected confirm his observations. "Is there something you wish me to do, sir?" he asked carefully. For a mad moment he wished the answer was yes.

Khy only sighed and eased herself back down into the chair, swung her feet up again. "If only," she said. "You go on, Loi. Your next shift here isn't for hours anyway, isn't it? Enjoy yourself."

Ruharn saluted and passed out of the bower. He headed next to his quarters, where he opened the case and unwrapped the dolls. "You'd better not be bombs," he told them. They didn't answer, which didn't make him feel better.

Dealing with bombs wasn't one of his skills, but if the dolls were what remained of the stolen children, that wasn't relevant. Besides, even if they were bombs, they were probably advanced foreigner bombs, and the fastness's scanners had failed to pick up on them when he brought them in.

The two dolls were nearly identical. Prodding one revealed that the hair was a wig, and beneath it the top of the skull came off. The head was hollow. The eyes, half-domes with luminous irises, were held in place by putty. Systematically, he took apart the rest of the doll. The doll was jointed, and elastic ran through channels in the body and limbs so that it could be posed.

As for the slag of bullets, they appeared to be real metal, not resin. He prodded them and jerked his hand back involuntarily. They were the exact temperature of his own skin. Feeling like a squeamish six-year-old, he pressed his fingertips against the resin just above the slag. The surface was cool; significantly cooler, in fact.

Logistical necessities, Ruharn thought, staring down at the dolls. Then he wrapped them back up, laid them carefully in the case, and put the case under his bed. Stupid hiding place, but it wasn't as if he had a better one. And anyway, the real hiding place was where he had kept it all these years, the pitted lump he had for a heart.

• • •

At the appointed time, Ruharn went to the Falcon Councilor's chambers. He did not wear his uniform. Lately she liked him to wear what the courtiers did, necklaces of twisted gold and fitted coats with their undulating lace, dark red brocades. He obliged her; he understood his function. The guards with their falcon insignia acknowledged him merely with nods, making no comment.

The councilor stood looking at a tapestry-of-labyrinths when he stopped just short of entering, the way she liked him to. "Madam," he said. In the very early days she had liked it when he knelt. Her mood varied, however, and he didn't care one way or another. If pride had been important to him, he wouldn't be here.

"Come in," she said in the clear sweet voice whose inflections he knew so well.

Ruharn came up behind her and undid, one-handed, the clasps and knots and chains that held her veil in place. She had told him once that she only wore it here; everywhere else it was the familiar falcon mask. Ruharn found it telling, although he did not say so, that the fastenings were more elaborate than the veil itself. He was no pauper, but a bolt of the fabric, with its infinitesimally shimmering threads and texture like moondrift silk, would have beggared him. He always had the disquieting feeling that his fingerprints would sully the fibers, leave scars deep as trenches and hideous as gangrene. But he didn't say that either.

"Your hands are cold," she murmured.

It always took him a while to undo all the fastenings. "Sorry," Ruharn said mildly, "but you didn't like my last pair of gloves and it's not as if I've had time to go shopping."

She didn't call him on the lie, and he bent to kiss the back of her head, inhaling the fragrance of her hair.

The veil fell away, drifting through the air like a feather, or a fall of light, or a flower's breath. Ruharn always felt ridiculous whisking it away to lay it on the councilor's dresser without folding it, but she had never complained. He lifted her hair, which was hooked through with crystal—it was getting near the time where she would have to tear off her face again—taking care not to tug the dark coils. Unhurriedly, he pressed his lips to the back of her neck, once, twice. Again. Her perfume smelled of dried roses and wood-of-pyres. Inhaling it made his heartbeat quicken. Reportedly she wore it only for her lovers.

"Tell me," he said right into her ear, "is it true what's been happening to the children lately?"

He wanted her to tell him the truth, however familiar; however horrible. If she told him the truth, he would accept his complicity and forget Merenne again. He had been doing exactly that for all these years, after all. Surely he had earned a little truth in exchange for the years they had spent together.

The councilor's laugh came more as a vibration against his chest than a sound, and her voice was teasing. "You'll have to be more specific than that, my dear. Are we talking about schools, or orphanages, or some incident involving crawfish-racing?" (Naheng's crawfish were surprisingly large and fast, or this game would have been less popular than it was.)

Ruharn heard the lie and was surprised by the force of his own rage. He brought his hands up and down and around. She cried out as she landed against the wall, hard, breath slammed out of her, her arm bent close to breaking in his grip. "Are the mercenaries harvesting the children now, or is it still you?" He added, "It's been a long time since I did hand-to-hand. I could still get the mechanics wrong. So think about your answer."

"Why does it matter to you?"

He broke her arm. She screamed.

No one came. She hadn't triggered an alarm, and the guards were used to noise.

"Madam," he said, very formally. She went very still, very quiet. "Answer the question."

"We haven't sent out the Gardeners since the mercenaries came," the Falcon Councilor said raggedly. "It's their doing this time around." And, in a different voice entirely: "I had always hoped you might hesitate a little before doing—this."

"Neither one of us has ever been under the illusion that this relationship was about love," Ruharn said. "Did the mercenaries say outright that they would be recruiting the children?"

"They didn't say, but we knew."

"Is it too late to send them away?"

"We've paid," she said. "They will give us what we paid for. Don't you think we considered that people powerful enough to save us would also be powerful enough to plunder us? To wreck our way of life? But it was either submit to our destruction or choose the chance of salvation."

Ruharn thought for a moment. "All right. Take me to the Garden."

The councilor's laugh was ugly. "It always comes down to this. It took you longer than most, at least. What, are you concerned that the mercenaries will destroy the supply before you get your chance at youth unending?"

Let her think what she wanted. "Madam," he said, "you have a lot of bones and breaking them all would take time I don't have. I would speak you fair, but I'm done with niceties. The Garden."

"You picked one hell of a time to stage a coup, lover," the Falcon Councilor said in a voice like winter stabbing.

Is that what you think this is? Ridiculous that he wanted her to believe better of him, yet there it was. "Shut up," he said evenly. She was silent after that. It had been a long time since he had been anything but deferential to her, except in bed when she required otherwise.

It was a long way to the Garden. Ruharn expected her to call for help after all, or try to escape. But she kept looking at him, her eyes pierced through with pain, and she did neither. Sometimes she drew in a breath that might have become a sob; but then she controlled herself. He tried not to think about what he'd done to her.

The Garden, when it opened up before them in a staggering splendor of chokingly humid air and pearlescent lights, was choked with children, newborn to ten or eleven years old. It was impossible to tell how many there were, or how big the Garden was. They were sprawled every which way, a spill of limbs and crooked necks and lolling heads, and from them grew red pulsating vines, and from the vines shone red murmuring fruits. Perhaps it would have been less overwhelming if the children had been neatly organized, stacked by height or size in rows. Probably not.

In spite of himself, Ruharn looked among the faces for some echo of Merenne's features. Some echo of his own. It was impossible to tell amid the red tangles.

"The raw liquor is effective," the Falcon Councilor said after giving him just enough time to confront the sight, "if that's what you're thinking, but painful. Dragon is the only one who imbibes it in that form, and Dragon is a little peculiar. I'm surprised you didn't just have me take you to the wine cellars."

"No," Ruharn said. "This is what I want."

"The other councilors won't stand for this, you know."

"They won't have to."

She still didn't understand. "When they come after you—" Tellingly, she didn't say *we*: he was almost certain it was deliberate.

"Forget that, this is *damage control*," Ruharn said savagely, resisting the temptation to hit her. Stupid, considering he had already broken her arm and threatened systematic torture. "You made a bargain you only half-understood and you sent children to die in the most wasteful way possible, without even the leadership of someone like General Khy so they'd have a chance. The mercenaries aren't providing any sort of generalship themselves and I trust you weren't assuming that a bunch of children that age were going to spontaneously turn up any convenient tactical geniuses to do the job."

"This is rich," the councilor retorted, "from someone who turned his back on those same children during all the years they were bought as fodder for the Garden. Or did you manage to lie to yourself about what wine it is I drink when I'm not in your arms?"

He flinched. "Oh yes," he said, "I would rather be fucking you than dealing with this. I'm not unaware of what I am." The red silken sheets, her fragrant skin, the coils of glossy hair. The marks her mouth of living crystal left on his skin. "But apparently even I have limits."

Ruharn removed his ceremonial knife and laid it on the floor. Then he stripped, aware of her staring even though his body was no secret to either of them. He picked up the knife again, squared his shoulders, and waded into the Garden.

For all the useless ornamentation on the knife's hilt and sheath, its blade was just fine. He had no intention of wasting further time plucking fruit or squeezing it into his mouth. Instead, he cut directly into a handful of vines and brought them, spurting livid red, up to his mouth.

She was right. It burned going down, and burned his skin too, not like fire (he knew something of fire) but like hopes crushed down to singularity nights. But he swallowed, and swallowed, and swallowed, even as he choked; even as the red fluid dribbled down his chin and soaked his clothes. When the spray slowed, he grabbed blindly and cut again, and again, and again.

"Ruharn!" the Falcon Councilor cried out behind him. "Ruharn, you have to stop, it's *too much*—"

Good to know that she wasn't interested in that particular perversion. At least with him. He kept drinking, unable to see although his eyes were wide open, so nauseated he couldn't even throw up. Finally he dropped the knife and sank to his knees, coughing out an ugly pink-tinged spray.

After a while he became aware of her hand on his shoulder. Her touch, too, burned with the sticky-slick traces of the fluid. He shivered. Her hand felt large, and he felt thin, small, vulnerable in a way that hadn't been true for years. He looked down, not at his own hands, but at his thighs and their scars, not all of which had been received in battle. Looked up. She was taller now, larger.

"Ruharn," she said in a wretched voice. "You look—I never imagine you'd ever looked so innocent. Except your eyes."

"Childhood isn't about innocence," Ruharn said, both cynically amused at the way she cringed at how high his voice was now, and hating the sound of it himself. "It's about being *powerless*."

She didn't contest the point.

"Your mercenary company," Ruharn said. "You must have a way of contacting them still. Tell them to take me next." He assumed it would be the fastest way, instead of wandering around in some city waiting for them to find him. "If children are the coin they desire."

"You're even more crazed than I thought you were if you think I'll do that."

Hell of a time for her to get maternal. "I'm not Khy," Ruharn said. "I didn't go to the nobles' battle schools, or to the collegium for strategists. But I know more than those children do. Because that's who the mercenaries are, aren't they? Our children, transformed. *Let me go.*" He shook off her hand and rose to his feet.

The Falcon Councilor rose as well. "You have no guarantee that you'll be anything more than a drone while you're up there as—as whatever you become," she said.

"Doesn't matter," he said. "If there's a chance I can do some good, I have to take it."

"Fine," she said, distant, formal. "You have my gratitude, General."

She drew out two bright-and-dark balls, no larger than Ruharn's fists, and whispered into them. He couldn't hear the words. Then she set them down, dry-eyed, and stepped back. A door ruptured the air above the balls.

You won't feel grateful for long, Ruharn thought. But he bent his head to her, and went.

In five months and twenty-four days, the mercenaries reclaimed sixty-three percent of Nasteng.

In the fifteen days after General Loi Ruharn vanished, the invaders were repulsed entirely.

General Khy's attempts to tally the mercenaries' losses in both phases of the campaign, as opposed to the enemies' losses, were blocked.

Merenne watched for Gardeners in all the years that followed, but never saw any. She made toys for her next grandchildren; there were a few. No dolls.

The final attack came not from the invaders, who were driven off in a scythe-surge of explosions, but from the newly-coordinated starflyers and groundswarmers. Their original task done, they needled toward the Garden and crashed into it, raising a pillar of fire and monstrous ash.

The councilors, who were in the midst of a victory celebration, had nothing left to fight with. Then, as their forces failed them, they fled one by one, except the Falcon Councilor. She and General Khy stayed in the command bower to the last, playing cards.

The Garden's protections were sundered. It lay with its ruined red-black mass of vines and charred, sunken skeletons like a sore jabbed open over and over. Nothing would ever grow there again.

Deep in the mass were two broken beacons and two collapsed mannequins, their uniforms fused to their skin. One was a woman, its face candle-melted entirely away. The other was a man, probably; hard to tell, given the damage. But the sutures holding its mouth shut from the inside had torn open, and it was smiling.

ABOUT THE AUTHOR

Yoon Ha Lee's works have appeared in *Lightspeed, Tor.com, Beneath Ceaseless Skies,* and *The Magazine of Fantasy and Science Fiction.* Her collection *Conservation of Shadows* came out in 2013 from Prime Books. Currently she lives in Louisiana with her family and has not yet been eaten by gators.

Ship's Brother
ALIETTE DE BODARD

You never liked your sister.

I know you tried your best; that you would stay awake at night thinking on filial piety and family duty; praying to your ancestors and the bodhisattva Quan Am to find strength; but that it would always come back to that core of dark thoughts within you, that fundamental fright you carried with you like a yin shadow in your heart.

I know, of course, where it started. I took you to the mind-ship—because I had no choice, because Khi Phach was away on some merchant trip to the Twenty-Third Planet—because you were a quiet and well-behaved son, and the birth-master would have attendants to take care of you. You had just turned eight—had stayed up all night for Tet, and shaken your head at the red envelopes, telling me you were no longer a child and didn't need money for toys and sweets.

When we disembarked from the shuttle, I had to pause—it was almost time for your sister to be born, and I felt my entire body had grown still—my lungs afire, my muscles seized up, and your sister in my womb stopping her incessant thrashing for a brief, agonizing moment. And I felt, as I always did during a contraction, my thoughts slipping away, down the birth canal to follow your sister; felt myself die, little by little, my self extinguishing itself like a flame.

Like all Minds, she was hungry for the touch of a human soul; entwined around my thoughts, and in her eagerness to be born, she was pushing outwards, dragging me with her—I remembered pictures and holos of post-birth bearers, their faces slack, their eyes empty, their thought-nets as pale as the waning moon, and for a moment—before my lips curled around the mantras of the birth-masters—I felt a sliver of ice in my heart, a hollow of fear within my belly—the thought that it could be me, that it would be me, that I wasn't strong enough . . .

And then it passed; and I stood, breathing hard, in the center of the mind-ship they had laid out for my daughter.

"Mommy?" you asked.

"I'm fine, child," I said, slowly—breathing in the miracle of air, struggling to string together words that made sense. "I'm fine."

We walked together to the heartroom, where the birth-master would be waiting for us. Within me, your sister was tossing and turning—throbbing incessantly, a beating heart, a pulsing machine, the weight of metal and optics within my womb. I ran my hands on the metal walls of the curving corridors, feeling oily warmth under my fingers—and your sister pulsed and throbbed and spoke within me, as if she were already eager to fly within the deep spaces.

You were by my side, watching everything with growing awe—silenced, for once, by the myriad red lanterns hung on rafters; by the holos in the corridors depicting scenes from *The Tale of Kieu* and *The Two Sisters in Exile;* by the characters gleaming on doors and walls—you ran everywhere, touched everything, laughing; and my heart seemed full of the sound of your voice.

The contractions were closer together, and the pain in my back never seemed to go away; from time to time, it would rack my entire body, and I bit my tongue not to cry out. The mantras were in my mind now; part of the incessant litany I kept whispering, over and over, to keep myself whole, to hold to the center of my being.

I had never prayed so hard in my entire life.

In the heartroom, the birth-master was waiting for us, with a cup of freshly brewed tea. I breathed in the flowery smell, watched the leaves dance within the shivering water—trying to remember what it felt to be light on my feet, to be free of pain and fatigue and nausea. "She's coming," I said, at last. I might have said something else, in other circumstances; made a comment from the Classic of Tea, quoted some poet like Nguyen Trai or Xuan Dieu; but my mind seemed to have deserted me.

"She is," the birth-master said, gravely. "It's almost over now, older aunt. You have to be strong."

I was; I tried; but it all slid like tears on polished jade. I was strong, but so was the Mind in my belly. And I could see other things in the room, too—the charms against death, and the bundle at the back of the room, which would hold the injector—they'd asked me what to do, should the birth go wrong, should I lose my mind, and I had told them I would rather die. It had seemed easy, at the time; but now that I stood facing a very real possibility it seemed very different.

I hadn't heard you for a while. When I looked up, you were still; watching the center of the room, utterly silent, utterly unmoving. "Mommy . . . "

It looked like a throne; if thrones could have protrusions and metal parts; and a geometry that seemed to continually reshape itself—like the spikes of a durian fruit, I'd thought earlier on, when they hadn't yet implanted your sister in my womb, but now it didn't feel quite so funny or innocuous. Now it was real.

"This is where the Mind comes to rest," the birth-master said. He laid a hand in the midst of the thing, into a hollow that seemed no bigger than a child's body. "As you see, all the proper connections are already in place." A mass of cables and fibres and sockets, and other things I couldn't recognize—all tangled together like a nest of snakes. "Your mommy will have to be very brave."

Another contraction racked through me, a wave that went from my womb to my back, stilling the world around us. I no longer felt huge or heavy; but merely detached, watching myself with growing anger and fear. This, now; this was real. Your sister would be born and plugged into the ship, and make it come alive; and I would have done my duty to the Emperor and to my ancestors. Else . . .

I vaguely heard the birth-master speak of courage again, and how I was the strongest woman he knew; and then the pain was back, and I doubled over, crying out.

"Mommy!"

"I'm—fine—" I whispered, trying to hold my belly—trying to keep myself still, to gather my thoughts together—she was strong and determined, your sister, hungry for life, hungry for her mother's touch.

"You're not fine," you said, and your voice suddenly sounded like that of an adult—grave and composed, and tinged with so much fear it brought me back to the world, for a brief moment.

I saw on the floor a puddle of blood that shone with the sheen of machine oil—how odd, I thought, before realizing that I was the one bleeding, the one dying piece by piece; and I was on the floor though I didn't remember kneeling, and the pain was flaring in my womb and in my back—and someone was screaming—I thought it was the birth-master, but it was me, it had always been me . . .

"Mommy," you said, from somewhere far away. "Mommy!" Your hands were wet with blood; and the birth-master's attendants were dragging you away, thank the ancestors. There were strong hands on me, whispering that I should hold, ride the crest of the pain, wait before I pushed, lest I lose myself altogether, scatter my own thoughts as your sister made her way out of my womb. My tongue was heavy with the repeated mantras, my lips bloodied where I had bit them; and I struggled to hold myself together, when all I longed for was to open up like a lotus flower; to scatter my thoughts like seeds upon the wind.

But through the haze of pain I saw you—saw, in the moment before the door closed upon you, the expression on your face; and I knew then that you'd never forget this, no matter how it all ended.

Of course, you never forgot, or forgave. Your sister was born safely; though I remained weak ever after, moving slowly through my own home, with bones that felt made of glass; and my thoughts always seemed to move sluggishly, as if part of me had really followed her out of the birth canal. But it all paled when they finally let me stand in the ship; when I felt it come to life under my feet; when I saw colors shift on the wall, and metal take on the sheen of oil; when the paintings slowly faded away, to be replaced by the lines of poetry I'd read to your sister in the womb—and when I heard a voice deeper than the emptiness of space whisper to me, "Mother."

The mind-ship was called *The Fisherman's Song*; and that became your sister's name; but in my heart she was always Mi Nuong, after the princess in the fairytale, the one who fell in love with her unseen fisherman.

But to you, she was the enemy.

You put away the Classics and the poets, and stole my books and holos about pregnancies and Minds—reading late at night, and asking me a thousand questions that I didn't always have the answer to. I thought you sought to understand your sister; but of course I was wrong.

I remember a day seven years after the birth—Khi Phach was away again to discuss shipments with some large suppliers, and you'd convinced me to have a banquet. You'd come to me in my office and told me that I shouldn't be so preoccupied with my husband and children. I almost laughed; but you looked so much in earnest, so concerned about me, that my whole body suddenly felt light, infused with warmth. "Of course, child," I said; and saw you smile, an expression that illuminated your entire being.

It was a huge banquet: in addition to our relatives, I'd invited my scholar classmates, and some of your friends so you wouldn't get bored. I'd expected you to wander off during the preparations, to find your friends or some assignment you absolutely had to study; but you didn't. You stood in the kitchen, fetching bits and pieces, and helping me make salad rolls and shrimp toasts—and mixed dipping sauces with such concentration, as if they were all that mattered in the world.

Your sister was there too—not physically present, but she'd linked herself to the house's com systems, and her translucent avatar stood in the kitchen: a smaller model of *The Fisherman's Song* that floated around the room, giving us instructions about the various recipes, and laughing when we tore rice papers or dashed across the room for a missing ingredient. For once, you seemed not to mind her presence; and everything in the household seemed . . . harmonious and ideal, the dream put forth by the Classics.

At the banquet, I was surprised to find you sitting at my table—it wasn't so much the breach of etiquette, I had never been over-concerned with such strictures, as something else. "Shouldn't you be with your friends?" I asked.

You glanced, carelessly, to the end of the room, where the younger people sat: candidates to the mandarin exams, like you; and a group of pale-skinned outsiders, who looked a bit dazed, doing their best to follow the conversations by their side. "I can be with them later," you said, making a dismissive gesture with your hands. "There's plenty of time."

"There's also plenty of time to be with me," I pointed out.

You pulled your chair, and sat down with a grimace. "Time passes," you said at last. "Mother . . . "

I laughed. "I'm not that frail." Though I felt weak that particular night, my bones and womb aching, as if in memory of giving birth to your sister; but I didn't tell you that.

"Of course you're not." You looked awkward, staring at your bowl as if you didn't know what to say anymore. Of course, you were fifteen—no adult yet, and ancestors know even Khi Phach had never mastered the art of small conversation.

I glanced at Mi Nuong. Your sister didn't eat; and so she spent the banquet at the back of the room, at a table with the avatars of other ships—knowing her, she'd be steering the conversation at the table to literature, and then disengage and listen to everyone's ideas. It seemed as though everything was going well; and I turned back to the people around my table.

After a while, I found myself deep in talk with Scholar Soi, one of my oldest friends from the Academy; and paying less attention to you, though you intervened from time to time in the discussion, bringing up a reference or a quotation you thought apt—you'd learnt your lessons well.

Soi beamed at you. "Wonderful boy. Ready to sit for your mandarin exams, I'd say."

You looked pale, then, as if you'd swallowed something that had got stuck in your throat. "I'm not sure, elder aunt."

"Modesty becomes you. Of course you're ready. The fear will go away once you're sitting in your exam cell, facing the dissertation subject." She smiled fondly at that. You still looked ill; and I resolved to speak to you afterwards, to tell you that you had nothing to fear.

"In fact," Soi said, "we should have something right here, right now. A poetry competition, to give everyone a chance to shine. What do you think, child?"

I'd expected you to say no; but you actually looked interested. If there was one thing you shared with your sister and with me, it was your love of words. "I'd be honored, elder aunt."

"Younger sister?" Soi asked me, but I shook my head.

I don't know how Soi did it, but she soon got most of the guests gathered around a table laden with wine cups—making florid gestures with her arms as she explained the rules. The outsiders, who didn't speak the language very well, had all declined, except for one; but it was still a sizeable audience. You stood at the forefront of it, eagerly hanging on to Soi's every word.

As Soi handed out turns for composing poetry, I found Mi Nuong hovering by my side. "I thought you'd be with them," I said.

"What about you, Mother?"

I sighed. "He's fifteen, and proud of his learning. He doesn't need to compete with his forty-year-old mother."

"Or with his sister." Mi Nuong's voice was uncannily serene; but of course, navigating the deep spaces, the odd dimensions that folded space back upon itself, she saw things we didn't.

"No," I said at last. I wasn't blind; and had seen the way you avoided her.

"It doesn't matter, Mother," Mi Nuong said, still in the same serene tones. "He'll come around."

"You sound like you can see the future."

"Of course not." She sounded amused. "It would be nice, though." She fell silent, then; and I knew what she was thinking: that she didn't need to see the future to know that she'd outlive us all. Minds lived for centuries.

"Don't—" I started, but she cut me off.

"Don't worry about me. It's not that bad. I have so many more things to worry about, it doesn't really loom large." She sighed—I knew she was lying to reassure me, but I didn't press the point. "Look at him. He's still such a child."

And she wasn't, not anymore—Minds didn't age or mature at the same rate as humans. Perhaps it was her physiology, perhaps it was the mere act of crossing deep spaces so often, but she sounded disturbingly adult; even older than I sometimes. "You can't hold him to your standards."

She laughed—girlish, carefree. "Of course not. He's human."

"But still your brother?" I asked.

"Don't be silly, Mother. Of course he's my brother. He's such an idiot sometimes, but then so am I. It's what ties us together." Her voice was brimming with fond amusement; and her avatar nudged slightly closer to me, to get a better view of the contest. Everyone was laughing now, as a very tipsy scholar attempted to compose a poem about autumn and wine, and mangled words. The lone outsider stood by your side, and didn't laugh: his eyes were dark and intent, and he had a hand on your shoulder as he spoke to you—it looked as if he was trying to reassure you, which I couldn't fault him for.

"He worries for nothing," Mi Nuong said. "He'll win with ease."

And, indeed, when your turn came, you got up, gently setting aside the outsider's hand—and made up a poem about crab-flowers, making puns and references to other poems effortlessly, as if it was all part of some inner flow you could dip into. People stood, silent, as if struck with awe; and then Soi bowed to you, as younger to elder, and everyone else started to crowd around you in order to give you congratulations.

"See? I told you. He'll fly through his examinations, get a mandarin posting wherever he wants," Mi Nuong said.

"Of course he will," I said. I'd never doubted it; never questioned that you had my talent for literature, and Khi Phach's cunning and practical intelligence.

I looked at you—at the way you stood with your arms splayed out, basking in the praise of scholars; at your face still flushed with the declaiming of poetry—and you looked back at me, and saw me sitting with your sister by my side; and your face darkened in that moment, became as brittle as thin ice.

I felt a shiver go down my spine—as if some dark spirit had touched me and cast a shadow over all the paths of my future.

But the shadow never seemed to materialize: you passed your mandarin exams with ease—and awaited a posting from the government, though you closeted yourself with your friends and wouldn't confide any of your plans to us.

The summer after your exams, we went to see Mi Nuong—you and me and Khi Phach, who had just returned from his latest expedition. We took a lift to the orbital that held the spaceport—watching the fractured continents of the Eighteenth planet recede to a string of pearls in the middle of the ocean.

You sat away from us, reading a book a friend had given you—the outsiders' *Planet of Danger and Desire,* which was the latest rage that summer—while Khi Phach and I watched the receding continents, and talked about the future and what it held in store for us.

At the docks, the screens blinked above us, showing that your sister had just arrived from the First Planet. We stood outside the gate, waiting for her passengers to disembark—a stream of Viets and Xuyans, wearing silk robes and shirts, their faces still tense from the journey—from the odd sounds and sights, and the queer distortions of metal and flesh and bones one experienced aboard a mind-ship in deep spaces.

There were dignitaries from the Court itself, in five-panel brocade, their topknots adorned with exquisite jade and gold, talking amongst themselves in quiet tones—and a group of saffron-cloaked monks carrying nothing but the clothes on their back, their faces calm and ageless, making me ache for their serenity. Last of all came a vacant-eyed mother who hadn't survived the birth of her Mind, being led by her husband like a small child. My hands must have tensed without my realizing it, because Khi Phach grabbed me so hard I felt bruised, and forced me to look away.

"It's over," he said. "You'll never need to carry another Mind again."

I looked at my hands, tracing the shape of my bones through translucent skin—it had never been the same since Mi Nuong's birth. "Yes. I guess it is."

When we turned back, you weren't with us. I glanced at Khi Phach, fighting rising panic: you were an adult after all, hardly likely to be defenseless or lost. "He must have gone to another dock," Khi Phach said.

We searched the docks; the shops; the entire concourse, even the pagodas set away from the confusion of the spaceport's crowd, before we finally found you.

You were at the back of the spaceport, where the outsider hibernation ships berthed—watching another stream of travelers, their pale skins glistening from the fluid in the hibernation cradles, their eyes still faraway, reeling from the shock of waking up—the knowledge that the thin thread of ansible communications was their only link to a home planet where everyone they had ever held dear had aged and died during the long journey.

Khi Phach called out your name. "Anh!"

You didn't turn; your eyes remained on the outsiders.

"You gave us quite a fright," I said, laying a hand on your shoulder, feeling the tension in every one of your muscles. I thought it was stress; worry at the new life that opened up for you as a mandarin. "Come, let's see your sister."

You were silent and sullen the entire way; watching Khi Phach introduce himself to the crewmember that guarded the access to the ship, telling him we were family—her face lit up, and she congratulated him on such a beautiful child. I'd expected you to grimace in jealousy, as you always did when your sister was mentioned; but you didn't even speak.

"Child?" I asked.

I felt you tense as we walked into the tunnel leading to your sister's body; as the walls became organic, as faint traceries of poetry started appearing, and a persistent hum rose into the background: your sister's heartbeat, reverberating through the entire ship.

"This is stupid," you said, as we entered.

"What is?" Khi Phach asked.

"Mind-ships." You shook your head. "It's not meant to be that way."

Khi Phach glanced at me, inquisitively; for once, I was stuck for words. "Outsiders do it better," you said, your hands shut into fists.

We stopped, in the middle of the entrance hall—rafters adorned with red lanterns, poetry about family reunions, your sister's way of welcoming us home—I knew she was listening, that she might be hurt, but it was too late to take this outside, as you'd no doubt intended all along. "Better?" I said, arching an eyebrow. "Leaving for years in hibernation, leaving everything they own behind?"

"They don't take mind-ships!" You weren't looking at me or Khi Phach; but at the walls, your sister's body wrapped all around you. "They don't go plunging into deep spaces where we were never meant to go, don't go gazing into things that make them insane—they don't—don't birth those monstrosities just to navigate space faster!"

There was silence, in the wake of your words. All I could think of was all that I'd ignored; the priests' books that you'd brought home, your trips to the nearby Sleeper Church, and your pale-skinned outsider friends—like the one who had spoken to you so intently at the banquet.

"Apologize to your sister," Khi Phach said.

"I won't."

His voice was cold. "You just called her an abomination."

"I don't care."

I let go of you, then; moved away with one hand over my heart, as if I could make the words go away. "Child. Apologize Please," I said, in the tone that I'd used when you were little.

"No." You laid a hand on the walls, feeling their warmth; and pulled back, as if burnt. "Look at you, Mother. All wasted up, for *her* sake. All our women, subjugated just so they can birth those things."

You sounded like Father Paul; like an outsider yourself, full of that same desperate rage and aggressiveness—though, unlike them, you had a home to come back to.

"I don't need you to defend me, child," I said. "And we can resume that discussion elsewhere—" I waved a hand, forestalling Khi Phach's objections— "but not here, not in your sister's hearing."

A wind rose through the ship, picking up sound as it whistled through empty rooms. "Abomination . . ." Mi Nuong whispered. "Come tell me what you think—to my face. In my heartroom."

You stared upwards; as if you could *see* her; guess at the mass of optics and flesh plugged into the ship—and before either of us could stop you, you spun and ran out of the ship, making small, convulsive noises that I knew were tears.

Child . . .

I would have run, too; but Khi Phach laid a hand on my shoulder. "Let him cool off first. You know you can't argue with him in that state."

"I'm sorry," I said to Mi Nuong.

The lights flickered; and the ship seemed to contract a little. "He's frightened," Mi Nuong said.

"Which is no excuse." Khi Phach's face was stern.

But he hadn't been there at the birth; he didn't remember what I remembered; the shadow that had lodged like a shard within your heart, that colored everything. "I should have seen it," I said. Because it was all my fault; because I should have never brought you to the ship that day. What had I been thinking, trusting in strangers to protect my own child?

"You shouldn't torment yourself," Mi Nuong said.

I laid a hand on a wall—watching lines of poetry scroll by, songs about fishermen flying cormorants over the river, about wars dashing beloved sons like strings of pearls—about the beauty of hibiscuses doomed to pass and become nothing, just as we, too, passed away and became nothing—and I thought about how small, how insignificant we were within the world—about letting go of grief and guilt. "I can't stop," I said. "He's my son, just as you are my daughter."

"I told you before. He'll see it."

"I guess," I said. "Tell me about your trip. How was it?"

She laughed; giggled like a teenage girl. "Wonderful. You should see the First Planet, it's so huge—it has all those palaces and gardens, covering it from end to end; and pagodas that go all the way through the atmosphere, joined to orbitals, so that prayers genuinely go out into the void . . . "

I remember it all; remember it vividly, every word, every nuance that happened that day. For, when we came home, you weren't there anymore.

You'd packed your things, and left a message. I guess you were a scholar in spite of everything, because you didn't send a mail through the terminal, but wrote it with pen and paper: crossed words over and over until they hardly made sense.

I can't live here anymore. I apologize for being an unfilial son; but I have to seek my fortune elsewhere.

Khi Phach started moving Heaven and Earth to find you; but I didn't have to look very far. Your name, barely disguised, was on the manifest for an outsider hibernation ship headed out of the Dai Viet Empire, to an isolated planet on the edge of a red sun—a trip sponsored by the Sleeper Church. The hibernation ship had left while we were still searching for you; and there was no calling it back, not without starting a war with the outsiders. And what pretext could we have given? You were an adult; sixteen already, with the mandarin exams behind you; old enough to do what you wanted with your life.

You wouldn't age in your hibernation pod; but by the time you arrived, twenty years would have elapsed for us, making the distance between us all but insurmountable.

Khi Phach fumed against the Church, speaking of retribution and judgment, making plans to bring this before the local magistrate. I merely stood still, watching the screen that showed the hibernation ship going further and further away from us—feeling as though someone had ripped my heart out of my chest.

Many years have passed, and you still haven't come back. Khi Phach took his anger and bitterness into his grave; and I stare at his holo every morning when I rise—wondering when I, too, will join him on the ancestral altar.

Your sister, of course, has hardly aged: Minds don't live like humans, and she'll survive us all. She's with me now—back from another trip into space, telling me about all the wonders she's seen. I ask about you; and feel the ship contracting around me—in sadness, in anger?

"I don't know, Mother. The outsider planets are closed to mind-ships."

I know it already, but I still ask.

"Have you—" I bite my lips, pull out the treacherous words one by one—"have you forgiven him?"

"Mother!" Mi Nuong laughs, gentle, carefree. "He was just a child when it happened. Why should I keep grudges that long? Besides . . . " Her voice is sadder, now.

"Yes," I say. "I've seen the holos, too." Gently, carefully, I pull your latest disk—finger it before triggering the ansible record it contains. An image of you hovers in the midst of the ship, transparent and leeched of colors.

"Mother. I hope this finds you well. I have started work for a newscast—this would please you, wouldn't it, my being a scholar after all?" You smile, but it doesn't reach all the way to your eyes; and your face is pale, as if you hadn't seen the sun in a long time. "I am well, though I think of you often."

The messages all come through ansible; so do money transfers—as if money could reduce the emptiness of space between us, as if it could repay me for your absence. "I was sorry to hear about Father. I miss you both terribly." You pause then, turn to look at something beyond the camera—I catch a glimpse of slim arms, wrapped around you—a quick hug, to give you strength, but even that doesn't light up your eyes or your face—before you look at the camera again. "I'm sorry. I—I wish I were home again."

I turn off the disk, let it lie on the floor—it becomes ringed with scrolling words, with poems of sorrow and loss.

"He's happy," Mi Nuong says, in a tone that makes clear she believes none of it. "Among the outsiders."

Walking on a strange land, in a strange world—learning new customs in an unfamiliar language—away from us, away from your family. "Happy," I say.

I finger the disk again. I know that if I turn it on again, I'll hear your final words, the ones that come at the end of the recording, spoken barely loud enough to be heard.

I miss you all terribly.

Us all. Father and Mother—and sister. This is the first time you've ever admitted this aloud. And I've seen the other, earlier holos; seen how your eyes become ringed with shadows as time passes; how unhappiness eats you alive, year after year, even as you tell me how good life is, among the outsiders.

I'll be long gone when your pain becomes heavier than your fear, heavier than your shame; when you turn away from your exile and return to the only place that was ever home to you. By the time you come back, I'll be dust, ashes spread in the void of space; one more portrait on the ancestral altar, to be honored and worshipped—I'll have passed on to another life, with the Buddha's blessing.

But I know, still, what will happen.

You'll walk out of the outsiders' docks, pale with the lack of sun, covered in the slime of your hibernation pod—shaking with the shock of awakening, your eyes filled with the same burning emptiness I remember so well, the same rage and grief that all you've ever held dear has been lost while you traveled.

And, like an answer to your most secret prayer, you'll find your sister waiting for you.

First published in *Interzone,* issue #241.

ABOUT THE AUTHOR

Aliette de Bodard is a software engineer who was born in the United States, but grew up in France, where she still lives. Only a few years into her career, her short fiction has appeared widely throughout the genre, and she has won the British SF Association Award for her story "The Shipmaker." Her novels include *Servant of the Underworld, Harbinger of the Storm,* and *Master of the House of Darts,* all recently reissued in a novel omnibus, *Obsidian and Blood.* Her most recent book is a chapbook novella, *On a Red Station, Drifting.*

Utriusque Cosmi
ROBERT CHARLES WILSON

Diving back into the universe (now that the universe is a finished object, boxed and ribboned from bang to bounce), Carlotta calculates ever-finer loci on the frozen ordinates of spacetime until at last she reaches a trailer park outside the town of Commanche Drop, Arizona. Bodiless, no more than a breath of imprecision in the Feynman geography of certain virtual particles, thus powerless to affect the material world, she passes unimpeded through a sheet-aluminum wall and hovers over a mattress on which a young woman sleeps uneasily.

The young woman is her own ancient self, the primordial Carlotta Boudaine, dewed with sweat in the hot night air, her legs caught up in a spindled cotton sheet. The bedroom's small window is cranked open, and in the breezeless distance a coyote wails.

Well, look at me, Carlotta marvels: skinny girl in panties and a halter, sixteen years old—no older than a gnat's breath—taking shallow little sleep-breaths in the moonlit dark. Poor child can't even see her own ghost. Ah, but she will, Carlotta thinks—she *must*.

The familiar words echo in her mind as she inspects her dreaming body, buried in its tomb of years, eons, kalpas. *When it's time to leave, leave. Don't be afraid. Don't wait. Don't get caught. Just go. Go fast.*

Her ancient beloved poem. Her perennial mantra. The words, in fact, that saved her life.

She needs to share those words with herself, to make the circle complete. Everything she knows about nature of the physical universe suggests that the task is impossible. Maybe so . . . but it won't be for lack of trying.

Patiently, slowly, soundlessly, Carlotta begins to speak.

Here's the story of the Fleet, girl, and how I got raptured up into it. It's all about the future—a bigger one than you believe in—so brace yourself.

It has a thousand names and more, but we'll just call it the Fleet. When I first encountered it, the Fleet was scattered from the core of the galaxy all through its spiraled tentacles of suns, and it had been there for millions of years, going about its business, though nobody on this planet knew anything about it. I guess every now and then a Fleet ship must have fallen to Earth, but it would have been indistinguishable from any common meteorite by the time it passed through the atmosphere: a chunk of carbonaceous chondrite smaller than a human fist, from which all evidence of ordered matter had been erased by fire—and such losses, which happened everywhere and often, made no discernable difference to the Fleet as a whole. All Fleet data (that is to say, all *mind*) was shared, distributed, fractal. Vessels were born and vessels were destroyed; but the Fleet persisted down countless eons, confident of its own immortality.

Oh, I know you don't understand the big words, child! It's not important for you to hear them—not *these* words—it's only important for me to *say* them. Why? Because a few billion years ago tomorrow, I carried your ignorance out of this very trailer, carried it down to the Interstate and hitched west with nothing in my backpack but a bottle of water, a half-dozen Tootsie Rolls, and a wad of twenty-dollar bills stolen out of Dan-O's old ditty bag. That night (tomorrow night: mark it) I slept under an overpass all by myself, woke up cold and hungry long before dawn, and looked up past a concrete arch crusted with bird shit into a sky so thick with falling stars it made me think of a dark skin bee-stung with fire. Some of the Fleet vectored too close to the atmosphere that night, no doubt, but I didn't understand that (any more than *you* do, girl)—I just thought it was a big flock of shooting stars, pretty but meaningless. And, after a while, I slept some more. And come sunrise, I waited for the morning traffic so I could catch another ride . . . but the only cars that came by were all weaving or speeding, as if the whole world was driving home from a drunken party.

"They won't stop," a voice behind me said. "Those folks already made their decisions, Carlotta. Whether they want to live or die, I mean. Same decision you have to make."

I whirled around, sick-startled, and that was when I first laid eyes on dear Erasmus.

Let me tell you right off that Erasmus wasn't a human being. Erasmus just then was a knot of shiny metal angles about the size of a microwave oven, hovering in mid-air, with a pair of eyes like the polished tourmaline they sell at those roadside souvenir shops. He didn't *have* to look that way—it was some old avatar he used because he figured that it would impress me. But I didn't know that then. I was only surprised, if that's not too mild a word, and too shocked to be truly frightened.

"The world won't last much longer," Erasmus said in a low and mournful voice. "You can stay here, or you can come with me. But choose quick, Carlotta, because the mantle's come unstable and the continents are starting to slip."

I half believed that I was still asleep and dreaming. I didn't know what that meant, about the mantle, though I guessed he was talking about the end of the world. Some quality of his voice (which reminded me of that actor Morgan Freeman) made me trust him despite how weird and impossible the whole conversation was. Plus, I had a confirming sense that *something* was going bad *somewhere,* partly because of the scant traffic (a Toyota zoomed past, clocking speeds it had never been built for, the driver a hunched blur behind the wheel), partly because of the ugly green cloud that just then billowed up over a row of rat-toothed mountains on the horizon. Also the sudden hot breeze. And the smell of distant burning. And the sound of what might have been thunder, or something worse.

"Go with you where?"

"To the stars, Carlotta! But you'll have to leave your body behind."

I didn't like the part about leaving my body behind. But what choice did I have, except the one he'd offered me? Stay or go. Simple as that.

It was a ride—just not the kind I'd been expecting.

There was a tremor in the earth, like the devil knocking at the soles of my shoes. "Okay," I said, "whatever," as white dust bloomed up from the desert and was taken by the frantic wind.

Don't be afraid. Don't wait. Don't get caught. Just go. Go fast.

Without those words in my head, I swear, girl, I would have died that day. Billions did.

She slows down the passage of time so she can fit this odd but somehow necessary monologue into the space between one or two of the younger Carlotta's breaths. Of course, she has no real voice in which to speak. The past is static, imperturbable in its endless sleep; molecules of air on their fixed trajectories can't be manipulated from the shadowy place where she now exists. Wake up with the dawn, girl, she says, steal the money you'll never spend—it doesn't matter; the important thing is to *leave.* It's time.

When it's time to leave, leave. Of all the memories she carried out of her earthly life, this is the most vivid: waking to discover a ghostly presence in her darkened room, a white-robed woman giving her the advice she needs at the moment she needs it. Suddenly Carlotta wants to scream the words: *When it's time to leave—*

But she can't vibrate even a single mote of the ancient air, and the younger Carlotta sleeps on.

Next to the bed is a thrift-shop night table scarred with cigarette burns. On the table is a child's night-light, faded cut-outs of Sponge-Bob Square-Pants pasted on the paper shade. Next to that, hidden under a splayed copy of *People* magazine, is the bottle of barbiturates Carlotta stole from Dan-O's ditty-bag this afternoon, the same khaki bag in which (she couldn't help but notice) Dan-O keeps his cash, a change of clothes, a fake driver's license, and a blue steel automatic pistol.

Young Carlotta detects no ghostly presence . . . nor is her sleep disturbed by the sound of Dan-O's angry voice and her mother's sudden gasp, two rooms away. Apparently, Dan-O is awake and sober. Apparently, Dan-O has discovered the theft. That's a complication.

But Carlotta won't allow herself to be hurried.

The hardest thing about joining the Fleet was giving up the idea that I had a body, that my body had a real place to be.

But that's what everybody believed at first, that we were still whole and normal—everybody rescued from Earth, I mean. Everybody who said "Yes" to Erasmus—and Erasmus, in one form or another, had appeared to every human being on the planet in the moments before the end of the world. Two and a half billion of us accepted the offer of rescue. The rest chose to stay put and died when the Earth's continents dissolved into molten magma.

Of course, that created problems for the survivors. Children without parents, parents without children, lovers separated for eternity. It was as sad and tragic as any other incomplete rescue, except on a planetary scale. When we left the Earth, we all just sort of re-appeared on a grassy plain as flat as Kansas and wider than the horizon, under a blue faux sky, each of us with an Erasmus at his shoulder and all of us wailing or sobbing or demanding explanations.

The plain wasn't "real," of course, not the way I was accustomed to things being real. It was a virtual place, and all of us were wearing virtual bodies, though we didn't understand that fact immediately. We kept on being what we expected ourselves to be—we even wore the clothes we'd worn when we were raptured up. I remember looking down at the pair of greasy second-hand Reeboks I'd found at the Commanche Drop Goodwill store, thinking: in Heaven? *Really?*

"Is there any place you'd rather be?" Erasmus asked with a maddening and clearly inhuman patience. "Anyone you need to find?"

"Yeah, I'd rather be in New Zealand," I said, which was really just a hysterical joke. All I knew about New Zealand was that I'd seen a show about it on PBS, the only channel we got since the cable company cut us off.

"Any particular part of New Zealand?"

"What? Well—okay, a beach, I guess."

I had never been to a real beach, a beach on the ocean.

"Alone, or in the company of others?"

"Seriously?" All around me people were sobbing or gibbering in (mostly) foreign languages. Pretty soon, fights would start to break out. You can't put a couple of billion human beings so close together under circumstances like that and expect any other result. But the crowd was already thinning, as people accepted similar offers from their own Fleet avatars.

"Alone," I said. "Except for *you.*"

And quick as that, there I was: Eve without Adam, standing on a lonesome stretch of white beach.

After a while, the astonishment faded to a tolerable dazzle. I took off my shoes and tested the sand. The sand was pleasantly sun-warm. Saltwater swirled up between my toes as a wave washed in from the coral-blue sea.

Then I felt dizzy and had to sit down.

"Would you like to sleep?" Erasmus asked, hovering over me like a gem-studded party balloon. "I can help you sleep, Carlotta, if you'd like. It might make the transition easier if you get some rest, to begin with."

"You can answer some fucking *questions,* is what you can *do!*" I said.

He settled down on the sand beside me, the mutant offspring of a dragonfly and a beach ball. "Okay, shoot," he said.

It's a read-only universe, Carlotta thinks. The Old Ones have said as much, so it must be true. And yet, she knows, she *remembers,* that the younger Carlotta will surely wake and find her here: a ghostly presence, speaking wisdom.

But how can she make herself perceptible to this sleeping child? The senses are so stubbornly material, electrochemical data cascading into vastly complex neural networks . . . is it possible she could intervene in some way at the borderland of quanta and perception? For a moment, Carlotta chooses to look at her younger self with different eyes, sampling the fine gradients of molecular magnetic fields. The child's skin and skull grow faint and then transparent as Carlotta shrinks her point of view and wanders briefly through the carnival of her own animal mind, the buzzing innerscape where skeins of dream merge and separate like fractal soap-bubbles. If she could manipulate even a single boson—influence the charge at some critical synaptic junction, say—

But she can't. The past simply doesn't have a handle on it. There's no uncertainty here anymore, no alternate outcomes. To influence the past would be to *change* the past, and, by definition, that's impossible.

The shouting from the next room grows suddenly louder and more vicious, and Carlotta senses her younger self moving from sleep toward an awakening, too soon.

Of course, I figured it out eventually, with Erasmus's help. Oh, girl, I won't bore you with the story of those first few years—they bored *me*, heaven knows.

Of course "heaven" is exactly where we weren't. Lots of folks were inclined to see it that way—assumed they must have died and been delivered to whatever afterlife they happened to believe in. Which was actually not *too* far off the mark: but, of course, God had nothing to do with it. The Fleet was a real-world business, and ours wasn't the first sentient species it had raptured up. Lots of planets got destroyed, Erasmus said, and the Fleet didn't always get to them in time to salvage the population, hard as they tried—we were *lucky*, sort of.

So I asked him what it was that caused all these planets to blow up.

"We don't know, Carlotta. We call it the Invisible Enemy. It doesn't leave a signature, whatever it is. But it systematically seeks out worlds with flourishing civilizations and marks them for destruction." He added, "It doesn't like the Fleet much, either. There are parts of the galaxy where we don't go—because if we *do* go there, we don't come back."

At the time, I wasn't even sure what a "galaxy" was, so I dropped the subject, except to ask him if I could see what it looked like—the destruction of the Earth, I meant. At first, Erasmus didn't want to show me; but after a lot of coaxing, he turned himself into a sort of floating TV screen and displayed a view "looking back from above the plane of the solar ecliptic," words which meant nothing to me.

What I saw was . . . well, no more little blue planet, basically.

More like a ball of boiling red snot.

"What about my mother? What about Dan-O?"

I didn't have to explain who these people were. The Fleet had sucked up all kinds of data about human civilization, I don't know how. Erasmus paused as if he was consulting some invisible Rolodex. Then he said, "They aren't with us."

"You mean they're dead?"

"Yes. Abby and Dan-O are dead."

But the news didn't surprise me. It was almost as if I'd known it all along, as if I had had a vision of their deaths, a dark vision to go along with that ghostly visit the night before, the woman in a white dress telling me *go fast*.

Abby Boudaine and Dan-O, dead. And me raptured up to robot heaven. Well, well.

"Are you sure you wouldn't like to sleep now?"

"Maybe for a while," I told him.

Dan-O's a big man, and he's working himself up to a major tantrum. Even now, Carlotta feels repugnance at the sound of his voice, that gnarl of angry consonants. Next, Dan-O throws something solid, maybe a clock, against the wall. The clock goes to pieces, noisily. Carlotta's mother cries out in response, and the sound of her wailing seems to last weeks.

"It's not good," Erasmus told me much later, "to be so much alone."

Well, I told him, I *wasn't* alone—he was with me, wasn't he? And he was pretty good company, for an alien machine. But that was a dodge. What he *meant* was that I ought to hook up with somebody human.

I told him I didn't care if ever set eyes on another human being ever again. What had the human race ever done for *me*?

He frowned—that is, he performed a particular contortion of his exposed surfaces that I had learned to interpret as disapproval. "That's entropic talk, Carlotta. Honestly, I'm worried about you."

"What could happen to me?" Here on this beach where nothing ever *really* happens, I did not add.

"You could go crazy. You could sink into despair. Worse, you could die."

"I could *die*? I thought I was immortal now."

"Who told you that? True, you're no longer *living*, in the strictly material sense. You're a metastable nested loop embedded in the Fleet's collective mentation. But everything's mortal, Carlotta. Anything can die."

I couldn't die of disease or falling off a cliff, he explained, but my "nested loop" was subject to a kind of slow erosion, and stewing in my own lonely juices for too long was liable to bring on the decay that much faster.

And, admittedly, after a month on this beach, swimming and sleeping too much and eating the food Erasmus conjured up whenever I was hungry (though I didn't really need to eat), watching recovered soap operas on his bellyvision screen or reading celebrity magazines (also embedded in the Fleet's collective memory) that would never get any fresher or produce another issue, and just being basically miserable as all hell, I thought maybe he was right.

"You cry out in your sleep," Erasmus said. "You have bad dreams."

"The world ended. Maybe I'm depressed. You think meeting people would help with that?"

"Actually," he said, "you have a remarkable talent for being alone. You're sturdier than most. But that won't save you, in the long run."

So I tried to take his advice. I scouted out some other survivors. Turned out, it was interesting what some people had done in their new incarnations as Fleet-data. The Erasmuses had made it easy for like-minded folks to find each other and to create environments to suit them. The most successful of these cliques, as they were sometimes called, were the least passive ones: the ones with a purpose. Purpose kept people lively. Passive cliques tended to fade into indifference pretty quickly, and the purely hedonistic ones soon collapsed into dense orgasmic singularities; but if you were curious about the world, and hung out with similarly curious friends, there was a lot to keep you thinking.

None of those cliques suited me in the long run, though. Oh, I made some friends, and I learned a few things. I learned how to access the Fleet's archival data, for instance—a trick you had to be careful with. If you did it right, you could think about a subject as if you were doing a Google search, all the relevant information popping up in your mind's eye just as if it had been there all along. Do it too often or too enthusiastically, though, and you ran the risk of getting lost in the overload—you might develop a "memory" so big and all-inclusive that it absorbed you into its own endless flow.

(It was an eerie thing to watch when it happened. For a while, I hung out with a clique that was exploring the history of the non-human civilizations that had been raptured up by the Fleet in eons past . . . until the leader of the group, a Jordanian college kid by the name of Nuri, dived down too far and literally fogged out. He got this look of intense concentration on his face, and, moments later, his body turned to wisps and eddies of fluid air and faded like fog in the sunlight. Made me shiver. And I had liked Nuri—I missed him when he was gone.)

But by sharing the effort, we managed to safely learn some interesting things. (Things the Erasmuses could have just *told* us, I suppose; but we didn't know the right questions to ask.) Here's a big for-instance: although every species was mortal after it was raptured up—every species eventually fogged out much the way poor Nuri had—there were actually a few very long-term survivors. By that, I mean individuals who had outlived their peers, who had found a way to preserve a sense of identity in the face of the Fleet's hypercomplex data torrent.

We asked our Erasmuses if we could meet one of these long-term survivors.

Erasmus said no, that was impossible. The Elders, as he called them, didn't live on our timescale. The way they had preserved themselves was by dropping out of realtime.

Apparently, it wasn't necessary to "exist" continuously from one moment to the next. You could ask the Fleet to turn you off for a day or a week, then turn you on again. Any moment of active perception was called a *saccade,* and you could space your saccades as far apart as you liked. Want to live a thousand years? Do it by living one second out of every million that passes. Of course, it wouldn't *feel* like a thousand years, subjectively; but a thousand years would flow by before you aged much. That's basically what the Elders were doing.

We could do the same, Erasmus said, if we wanted. But there was a price tag attached to it. "Timesliding" would carry us incomprehensibly far into a future nobody could predict. We were under continual attack by the Invisible Enemy, and it was possible that the Fleet might lose so much cohesion that we could no longer be sustained as stable virtualities. We wouldn't get a long life out of it, and we might well be committing a kind of unwitting suicide.

"You don't really go anywhere," Erasmus summed up. "In effect, you just go fast. I can't honestly recommend it."

"Did I ask for your advice? I mean, what *are* you, after all? Just some little fragment of the Fleet mind charged with looking after Carlotta Boudaine. A cybernetic babysitter."

I swear to you, he looked *hurt.* And I heard the injury in his voice.

"I'm the part of the Fleet that cares about you, Carlotta."

Most of my clique backed down at that point. Most people aren't cut out to be timesliders. But I was more tempted than ever. "You can't tell me what to do, Erasmus."

"I'll come with you, then," he said. "If you don't mind."

It hadn't occurred to me that he might *not* come along. It was a scary idea. But I didn't let that anxiety show.

"Sure, I guess that'd be all right," I said.

• • •

Enemies out there too, the elder Carlotta observes. A whole skyful of them. As above, so below. Just like in that old drawing—what was it called? *Utriusque cosmi.* Funny what a person remembers. Girl, do you hear your mother crying?

The young Carlotta stirs uneasily in her tangled sheet.

Both Carlottas know their mother's history. Only the elder Carlotta can think about it without embarrassment and rage. Oh, it's an old story. Her mother's name is Abby. Abby Boudaine dropped out of high school pregnant, left some dreary home in South Carolina to go west with a twenty-year-old boyfriend who abandoned her outside Albuquerque. She gave birth in a California emergency ward and nursed Carlotta in a basement room in the home of a retired couple, who sheltered her in exchange for housework until Carlotta's constant wailing got on their nerves. After that, Abby hooked up with a guy who worked for a utility company and grew weed in his attic for pin money. The hookup lasted a few years, and might have lasted longer, except that Abby had a weakness for what the law called "substances," and couldn't restrain herself in an environment where coke and methamphetamine circulated more or less freely. A couple of times, Carlotta was bounced around between foster homes while Abby Boudaine did court-mandated dry-outs or simply binged. Eventually, Abby picked up ten-year-old Carlotta from one of these periodic suburban exiles and drove her over the state border into Arizona, jumping bail. "We'll never be apart again," her mother told her, in the strained voice that meant she was a little bit high or hoping to be. "Never again!" Blessing or curse? Carlotta wasn't sure which. "You'll never leave me, baby. You're my one and only."

Not such an unusual story, the elder Carlotta thinks, though her younger self, she knows, feels uniquely singled out for persecution.

Well, child, Carlotta thinks, try living as a distributed entity on a Fleet that's being eaten by invisible monsters, *then* see what it feels like.

But she knows the answer to that. It feels much the same.

"Now you *steal* from me?" Dan-O's voice drills through the wall like a rusty auger. Young Carlotta stirs and whimpers. Any moment now, she'll open her eyes, and then what? Although this is the fixed past, it feels suddenly unpredictable, unfamiliar, dangerous.

Erasmus came with me when I went timesliding, and I appreciated that, even before I understood what a sacrifice it was for him.

Early on, I asked him about the Fleet and how it came to exist. The answer to that question was lost to entropy, he said. He had never known a time without a Fleet—he couldn't have, because Erasmus *was* the Fleet, or at least a sovereign fraction of it.

"As we understand it," he told me, "the Fleet evolved from networks of self-replicating data-collecting machine intelligences, no doubt originally created by some organic species, for the purpose of exploring interstellar space. Evidence suggests that we're only a little younger than the universe itself."

The Fleet had outlived its creators. "Biological intelligence is unstable over the long term," Erasmus said, a little smugly. "But out of that original compulsion to acquire and share data, we evolved and refined our own collective purpose."

"That's why you hoover up doomed civilizations? So you can catalogue and study them?"

"So they won't be *forgotten,* Carlotta. That's the greatest evil in the universe—the entropic decay of organized information. Forgetfulness. We despise it."

"Worse than the Invisible Enemy?"

"The Enemy is evil to the degree to which it abets entropic decay."

"Why does it want to do that?"

"We don't know. We don't even understand what the Enemy *is,* in physical terms. It seems to operate outside of the material universe. If it consists of matter, that matter is non-baryonic and impossible to detect. It pervades parts of the galaxy—though not *all* parts—like an insubstantial gas. When the Fleet passes through volumes of space heavily infested by the Enemy, our loss-rate soars. And as these infested volumes of space expand, they encompass and destroy life-bearing worlds."

"The Enemy's growing, though. And the Fleet isn't."

I had learned to recognize Erasmus's distress, not just because he was slowly adopting somewhat more human features. "The Fleet is my home, Carlotta. More than that. It's my body, my heart."

What he didn't say was that by joining me in the act of surfing time, he would be isolating himself from the realtime network that had birthed and sustained him. In realtime, Erasmus was a fraction of something reassuringly immense. But in slide-time, he'd be as alone as an Erasmus could get.

And yet, he came with me, when I made my decision. He was *my* Erasmus as much as he was the Fleet's, and he came with me. What would you call that, girl? Friendship? At least. I came to call it love.

The younger Carlotta has stolen those pills (the ones hidden under her smudged copy of *People*) for a reason. To help her sleep, was what she told herself. But she didn't really have trouble sleeping. No: if she was honest, she'd have to say the pills were an escape hatch. Swallow enough of them, and it's, hey, fuck you, world! Less work than the highway, an alternative she was also considering.

More shouting erupts in the next room. A real roust-up, bruises to come. Then, worse, Dan-O's voice goes all small and jagged. That's a truly bad omen, Carlotta knows. Like the smell of ozone that floods the air in advance of a lightning strike, just before the voltage ramps up and the current starts to flow.

Erasmus built a special virtuality for him and me to time-trip in. Basically, it was a big comfy room with a wall-sized window overlooking the Milky Way.

The billions of tiny dense components that made up the Fleet swarmed at velocities slower than the speed of light, but timesliding made it all seem faster—scarily so. Like running the whole universe in fast-forward, knowing you can't go back. During the first few months of our expanded Now, we soared a long way out of the spiral arm that contained the abandoned Sun. The particular sub-swarm of the Fleet that hosted my sense of self was on a long elliptical orbit around the supermassive black hole at the galaxy's core, and from this end of the ellipse, over the passing days, we watched the Milky Way drop out from under us like a cloud of luminous pearls.

When I wasn't in that room, I went off to visit other timesliders, and some of them visited me there. We were a self-selected group of radical roamers with a thing for risk, and we got to know one another pretty well. Oh, girl, I wish I could tell you all the friends I made among that tribe of self-selected exiles! Many of them human, not all: I met a few of the so-called Elders of other species, and managed to communicate with them on a friendly basis. Does that sound strange to you? I guess it is. Surpassing strange. I thought so too, at first. But these were people (mostly people) and things (but things can be people too) that I mostly liked and often loved, and they loved me back. Yes, they did. Whatever quirk of personality made us timesliders drew us together against all the speedy dark outside our virtual walls. Plus—well, we were survivors. It took not much more than a month to outlive all the remaining remnant of humanity. Even our ghosts were gone, in other words, unless you counted *us* as ghosts.

Erasmus was a little bit jealous of the friends I made. He had given up a lot for me, and maybe I ought to have appreciated him more for it. Unlike us formerly biological persons, though, Erasmus maintained a tentative link with realtime. He had crafted protocols to keep himself current on changes in the Fleet's symbol-sets and core mentation. That way, he could update us on what the Fleet was doing—new species raptured up from dying worlds and so forth. None of these newcomers lasted long, though, from our lofty perspective, and I once asked Erasmus why the Fleet even bothered with such ephemeral creatures as (for instance) human beings. He said that every species was doomed in the long run, but that didn't make it okay to kill people—or to abandon them when they might be rescued. That instinct was what made the Fleet a moral entity, something more than just a collection of self-replicating machines.

And it made *him* more than a nested loop of complex calculations. In the end, Carlotta, I came to love Erasmus best of all.

Meanwhile the years and stars scattered in our wake like dust—a thousand years, a hundred thousand, a million, more, and the galaxy turned like a great white wheel. We all made peace with the notion that we were the last of our kind, whatever "kind" we represented.

If you could hear me, girl, I guess you might ask what I found in that deep well of strangeness that made the water worth drinking. Well, I found friends, as I said—isn't that enough? And I found lovers. Even Erasmus began to adopt a human avatar, so we could touch each other in the human way.

I found, in plain words, a *home,* Carlotta, however peculiar in its nature—a *real* home, for the first time in my life.

Which is why I was so scared when it started to fall apart.

In the next room, Abby isn't taking Dan-O's anger lying down. It's nearly the perfect storm tonight—Dan-O's temper and Abby's sense of violated dignity both rising at the same ferocious pitch, rising toward some unthinkable crescendo.

But her mother's outrage is fragile, and Dan-O is frankly dangerous. The young Carlotta had known that about him from the get-go, from the first time her mother came home with this man on her arm: knew it from his indifferent eyes and his mechanical smile; knew it from the prison tattoos he didn't bother to disguise and the boastfulness with which he papered over some hole in his essential self. Knew it from the meth-lab stink that burned off him like a chemical perfume. Knew it from the company he kept, from the shitty little deals with furtive men arranged in Carlotta's mother's home because his own rental bungalow was littered with incriminating cans of industrial solvent. Knew it most of all by the way he fed Abby Boudaine crystal meth in measured doses, to keep her wanting it, and by the way Abby began to sign over her weekly Wal-Mart paycheck to him like a dutiful servant, back when she was working checkout.

Dan-O is tall, wiry, and strong despite his vices. The elder Carlotta can hear enough to understand that Dan-O is blaming Abby for the theft of the barbiturates—an intolerable sin, in Dan-O's book. Followed by Abby's heated denials and the sound of Dan-O's fists striking flesh. All this discovered, not remembered: the young Carlotta sleeps on, though she's obviously about to wake; the critical moment is coming fast. And Carlotta thinks of what she saw when she raided Dan-O's ditty bag, the blue metal barrel with a black gnurled grip, a thing she had stared at, hefted, but ultimately disdained.

We dropped back down the curve of that elliptic, girl, and suddenly the Fleet began to vanish like drops of water on a hot griddle. Erasmus saw it first, because of what he was, and he set up a display so I could see it too: Fleet-swarms set as ghostly dots against a schema of the galaxy, the ghost-dots dimming perilously and some of them blinking out altogether. It was a graph of a massacre. "Can't anyone stop it?" I asked.

"They would if they could," he said, putting an arm (now that he had grown a pair of arms) around me. "They will if they can, Carlotta."

"Can *we* help?"

"We are helping, in a way. Existing the way we do means they don't have to use much mentation to sustain us. To the Fleet, we're code that runs a calculation for a few seconds out of every year. Not a heavy burden to carry."

Which was important, because the Fleet could only sustain so much computation, the upper limit being set by the finite number of linked nodes. And that number was diminishing as Fleet vessels were devoured wholesale.

"Last I checked," Erasmus said (which would have been about a thousand years ago, realtime), "the Fleet theorized that the Enemy is made of dark matter." (Strange stuff that hovers around galaxies, invisibly—it doesn't matter, girl; take my word for it; you'll understand it one day.) "They're not material objects so much as *processes*—parasitical protocols played out in dark matter clouds. Apparently, they can manipulate quantum events we don't even see."

"So we can't defend ourselves against them?"

"Not yet. No. And you and I might have more company soon, Carlotta. As long-timers, I mean."

That was because the Fleet continued to rapture up dying civilizations, nearly more than their shrinking numbers could contain. One solution was to shunt survivors into the Long Now along with us, in order to free up computation for battlefield maneuvers and such.

"Could get crowded," he warned.

"If a lot of strangers need to go Long," I said . . .

He gave me a carefully neutral look. "Finish the thought."

"Well . . . can't we just . . . go Longer?"

Fire a pistol in a tin box like this ratty trailer and the sound is ridiculously loud. Like being spanked on the ear with a two-by-four. It's the pistol shot that finally wakes the young Carlotta. Her eyelids fly open like window shades on a haunted house.

This isn't how the elder Carlotta remembers it. *Gunshot?* No, there was no *gunshot*: she just came awake and saw the ghost—

And no ghost, either. Carlotta tries desperately to speak to her younger self, wills herself to succeed, and fails yet again. So who fired that shot, and where did the bullet go, and why can't she *remember* any of this?

The shouting in the next room has yielded up a silence. The silence becomes an eternity. Then Carlotta hears the sound of footsteps—she can't tell whose—approaching her bedroom door.

In the end, almost every conscious function of the Fleet went Long, just to survive the attrition of the war with the dark-matter beings. The next loop through the galactic core pared us down to a fraction of what we used to be. When I got raptured up, the Fleet was a distributed cloud of baseball-sized objects running quantum computations on the state of their own dense constituent atoms—*millions and millions* of such objects, all linked together in a nested hierarchy. By the time we orbited back up our ellipsis, you could have counted us in the thousands, and our remaining links were carefully narrowbanded to give us maximum stealth.

So us wild timesliders chose to go Longer.

Just like last time, Erasmus warned me that it might be a suicidal act. If the Fleet was lost, we would be lost along with it . . . our subjective lives could end within days or hours. If, on the other hand, the Fleet survived and got back to reproducing itself, well, we might live on indefinitely—even drop back into realtime if we chose to do so. "Can you accept the risk?" he asked.

"Can *you?*"

He had grown a face by then. I suppose he knew me well enough to calculate what features I'd find pleasing. But it wasn't his ridiculous fake humanity I loved. What I loved was what went on behind those still-gemlike tourmaline eyes—the person he had become by sharing my mortality. "I accepted that risk a long time ago," he said.

"You and me both, Erasmus."

So we held on to each other and just—*went fast.*

Hard to explain what made that time-dive so vertiginous, but imagine centuries flying past like so much dust in a windstorm! It messed up our sense of *place,* first of all. Used to be we had a point of view light-years wide and deep . . . now all those loops merged into one continuous cycle; we grew as large as the Milky Way itself, with Andromeda bearing down on us like a silver armada. I held Erasmus in my arms, watching wide-eyed while he updated himself on the progress of the war and whispered new discoveries into my ear.

The Fleet had worked up new defenses, he said, and the carnage had slowed; but our numbers were still dwindling.

I asked him if we were dying.

He said he didn't know. Then he looked alarmed and held me tighter. "Oh, Carlotta . . . "

"What?" I stared into his eyes, which had gone faraway and strange. "*What is it?* Erasmus, tell me!"

"The Enemy," he said in numbed amazement.

"What about them?"

"*I know what they are.*"

The bedroom door opens.

The elder Carlotta doesn't remember the bedroom door opening. None of this is as she remembers it should be. The young Carlotta cringes against the backboard of the bed, so terrified she can barely draw breath. *Bless you, girl, I'd hold your hand if I could!*

What comes through the door is just Abby Boudaine. Abby in a cheap white nightgown. But Abby's eyes are yellow-rimmed and feral, and her nightgown is spattered with blood.

See, the thing is this. All communication is limited by the speed of light. But if you spread your saccades over time, that speed-limit kind of expands. Slow as we were, light seemed to cross galactic space in a matter of moments. Single thoughts consumed centuries. We felt the supermassive black hole at the center of the galaxy beating like a ponderous heart. We heard whispers from nearby galaxies, incomprehensibly faint but undeniably manufactured. Yes, girl, we were *that* slow.

But the Enemy was even slower.

"Long ago," Erasmus told me, channeling this information from the Fleet's own dying collectivity, "long ago, the Enemy learned to parasitize dark matter . . . to use it as a computational substrate . . . to evolve *within* it . . . "

"*How* long ago?"

His voice was full of awe. "Longer than you have words for, Carlotta. They're older than the universe itself."

Make any sense to you? I doubt it would. But here's the thing about our universe: it oscillates. It *breathes,* I mean, like a big old lung, expanding and shrinking and expanding again. When it shrinks, it wants to turn into a singularity, but it can't do that, because there's a limit to how much mass a quantum of volume can hold without busting. So it all bangs up again, until it can't accommodate any more emptiness. Back and forth, over and over. Perhaps, *ad infinitum.*

Trouble is, no information can get past those hot chaotic contractions. Every bang makes a fresh universe, blank as a chalkboard in an empty schoolhouse . . .

Or so we thought.

But dark matter has a peculiar relationship with gravity and mass, Erasmus said; so when the Enemy learned to colonize it, they found ways to propagate themselves from one universe to the next. They could survive *the end of all things material,* in other words, and they had already done so—many times!

The Enemy was genuinely immortal, if that word has any meaning. The Enemy conducted its affairs not just across galactic space, but across the voids that separate galaxies, clusters of galaxies, superclusters . . . slow as molasses, they were, but vast as all things, and as pervasive as gravity, and very powerful.

"So what have they got against the Fleet, if they're so big and almighty? Why are they killing us?"

Erasmus smiled then, and the smile was full of pain and melancholy and an awful understanding. "But they're not *killing* us, Carlotta. They're rapturing us up."

One time in school, when she was trying unsuccessfully to come to grips with *The Merchant of Venice,* Carlotta had opened a book about Elizabethan drama to a copy of an old drawing called *Utriusque Cosmi.* It was supposed to represent the whole cosmos, the way people thought of it back in Shakespeare's time, all layered and orderly: stars and angels on top, hell beneath, and a naked guy stretched foursquare between divinity and damnation. Made no sense to her at all. Some antique craziness. She thinks of that drawing now, for no accountable reason. *But it doesn't stop at the angels, girl. I learned that lesson. Even angels have angels, and devils dance on the backs of lesser devils.*

Her mother in her bloodstained nightgown hovers in the doorway of Carlotta's bedroom. Her unblinking gaze strafes the room until it fixes at last on her daughter. Abby Boudaine might be standing right here, Carlotta thinks, but those eyes are looking out from someplace deeper and more distant and far more frightening.

The blood fairly drenches her. But it isn't Abby's blood.

"Oh, Carlotta," Abby says. Then she clears her throat, the way she does when she has to make an important phone call or speak to someone she fears. "Carlotta . . . "

And Carlotta (the invisible Carlotta, the Carlotta who dropped down from that place where the angels dice with eternity) understands what Abby is about to say, recognizes at last the awesome circularity, not a paradox at all. She pronounces the words silently as Abby makes them real: "Carlotta. Listen to me, girl. I don't guess you understand any of this. I'm so sorry. I'm sorry for many things. But listen now. When it's time to leave, you leave. Don't be afraid, and don't get caught. Just go. Go *fast.*"

Then she turns and leaves her daughter cowering in the darkened room.

Beyond the bedroom window, the coyotes are still complaining to the moon. The sound of their hooting fills up the young Carlotta's awareness until it seems to speak directly to the heart of her.

Then comes the second and final gunshot.

I have only seen the Enemy briefly, and by that time, I had stopped thinking of them as the Enemy.

Can't describe them too well. Words really do fail me. And by that time, might as well admit it, I was not myself a thing I would once have recognized as human. Just say that Erasmus and I and the remaining timesliders were taken up into the Enemy's embrace along with all the rest of the Fleet—all the memories we had deemed lost to entropy or warfare were preserved there. The virtualities the Enemies had developed across whole kalpas of time were labyrinthine, welcoming, strange beyond belief. Did I roam in those mysterious glades? Yes I did, girl, and Erasmus by my side, for many long (subjective) years, and we became—well, larger than I can say.

And the galaxies aged and flew away from one another until they were swallowed up in manifolds of cosmic emptiness, connected solely by the gentle and inexorable thread of gravity. Stars winked out, girl; galaxies merged and filled with dead and dying stars; atoms decayed to their last stable forms. But the fabric of space can tolerate just so much emptiness. It isn't infinitely elastic. Even vacuum ages. After some trillions and trillions of years, therefore, the expansion became a contraction.

During that time, I occasionally sensed or saw the Enemy—but I have to call them something else: say, *the Great Old Ones,* pardon my pomposity—who had constructed the dark matter virtualities in which I now lived. They weren't people at all. Never were. They passed through our adopted worlds like storm clouds, black and majestic and full of subtle and inscrutable lightnings. I couldn't speak to them, even then; as large and old as I had become, I was only a fraction of what they were.

I wanted to ask them why they had destroyed the Earth, why so many people had to be wiped out of existence or salvaged by the evolved benevolence of the Fleet. But Erasmus, who delved into these questions more deeply than I was able to, said the Great Old Ones couldn't perceive anything as tiny or ephemeral as a rocky planet like the Earth. The Earth and all the many planets like her had been destroyed, not by any willful calculation, but by autonomic impulses evolved over the course of many cosmic conflations—impulses as imperceptible and involuntary to the Old Ones as the functioning of your liver is to *you,* girl.

The logic of it is this: Life-bearing worlds generate civilizations that eventually begin playing with dark matter, posing a potential threat to the continuity of the Old Ones. Some number of these intrusions can be tolerated and contained—like the Fleet, they were often an enriching presence—but too many of them would endanger the stability of the system. It's as if we were germs, girl, wiped out by a giant's immune system. They couldn't *see* us, except as a somatic threat. Simple as that.

But they could see the *Fleet.* The Fleet was just big enough and durable enough to register on the senses of the Old Ones. And the Old Ones weren't malevolent: they perceived the Fleet much the way the Fleet had once perceived *us,* as something primitive but alive and thinking and worth the trouble of salvation.

So they raptured up the Fleet (and similar Fleet-like entities in countless other galaxies), thus preserving us against the blind oscillations of cosmic entropy.

(Nice of them, I suppose. But if I ever grow large enough or live long enough to confront an Old One face to face, I mean to lodge a complaint. Hell *yes* we were small—people are some of the smallest thought-bearing creatures in the cosmos, and I think we all kind of knew that even before the end of the world . . . *you* did, surely. But pain is pain and grief is grief. It might be inevitable, it might even be built into the nature of things; but it isn't *good*, and it ought not to be tolerated, if there's a choice.)

Which I guess is why I'm here watching you squinch your eyes shut while the sound of that second gunshot fades into the air.

Watching you process a nightmare into a vision.

Watching you build a pearl around a grain of bloody truth.

Watching you *go fast*.

The bodiless Carlotta hovers a while longer in the fixed and changeless corridors of the past.

Eventually, the long night ends. Raw red sunlight finds the window.

Last dawn this small world will ever see, as it happens; but the young Carlotta doesn't know that yet.

Now that the universe has finished its current iteration, all its history is stored in transdimensional metaspace like a book on a shelf—it can't be changed. Truly so. I guess I know that now, girl. Memory plays tricks that history corrects.

And I guess that's why the Old Ones let me have access to these events, as we hover on the brink of a new creation.

I know some of the questions you'd ask me if you could. You might say, *Where are you really?* And I'd say, *I'm at the end of all things, which is really just another beginning.* I'm walking in a great garden of dark matter, while all things known and baryonic spiral up the ladder of unification energies to a fiery new dawn. I have grown so large, girl, that I can fly down history like a bird over a prairie field. But I cannot remake what has already been made. That is one power I do not possess.

I watch you get out of bed. I watch you dress. Blue jeans with tattered hems, a man's lumberjack shirt, those thrift-shop Reeboks. I watch you go to the kitchen and fill your vinyl Bratz backpack with bottled water and Tootsie Rolls, which is all the cuisine your meth-addled mother has left in the cupboards.

Then I watch you tiptoe into Abby's bedroom. I confess I don't remember this part, girl. I suppose it didn't fit my fantasy about a benevolent ghost. But here you are, your face fixed in a willed indifference, stepping over Dan-O's corpse. Dan-O bled a lot after Abby Boudaine blew a hole in his chest, and the carpet is a sticky rust-colored pond.

I watch you pull Dan-O's ditty bag from where it lies half under the bed. On the bed, Abby appears to sleep. The pistol is still in her hand. The hand with the pistol in it rests beside her head. Her head is damaged in ways the young Carlotta can't stand to look at. Eyes down, girl. That's it.

I watch you pull a roll of bills from the bag and stuff it into your pack. Won't need that money where you're going! But it's a wise move, taking it. Commendable forethought.

Now go.

I have to go too. I feel Erasmus waiting for me, feel the tug of his love and loyalty, gentle and inevitable as gravity. He used to be a machine older than the dirt under your feet, Carlotta Boudaine, but he became a man—*my* man, I'm proud to say. He needs me, because it's no easy thing crossing over from one universe to the next. There's always work to do, isn't that the truth?

But right now, you go. You leave those murderous pills on the nightstand, find that highway. Don't be afraid. Don't wait. Don't get caught. Just go. Go fast. And excuse me while I take my own advice.

First published in *The New Space Opera 2,*
edited by Gardner Dozois & Jonathan Strahan.

ABOUT THE AUTHOR

Robert Charles Wilson made his first sale in 1974, but little more was heard from him until the late '80s, when he began to publish a string of ingenious and well-crafted novels and stories that have since established him among the top ranks of the writers who came to prominence in the last two decades of the 20th Century. His first novel, *A Hidden Place,* appeared in 1986. He won the John W. Campbell Memorial Award for his novel *The Chronoliths,* the Philip K. Dick Award for his novel *Mysterium,* and the Aurora Award for his story "The Perseids." In 2006, he won the Hugo Award for his acclaimed novel, *Spin.* His other books include the novels *Memory Wire, Gypsies, The Divide, The Harvest, A Bridge of Years, Darwinia, Blind Lake, Bios, Axis,* and *Julian Comstock: A Story of 22nd-Century America,* and a collection of his short work, *The Perseids and Other Stories.* His most recent book is the novel, *Burning Paradise.* He lives in Toronto, Canada.

Distributed Cities
CARL ABBOTT

The Swarm is a fleet of at least one hundred fifty dirigibles that cease-lessly crisscross their planet in the recent action-packed novel *Terminal World* by Alastair Reynolds. Once they were the defense force for the vast city of Spearpoint, but they along ago declared independence and have become a complete society. In effect, they constitute the physically disconnected pieces of a single city.

Reynolds does not supply full details, but it is clear that different airships serve different functions, much like the neighborhoods or districts of a city. An oversized super-aerostat serves as the city's "downtown" and government center. There are military airships, and presumably industrial and agricultural airships to serve the different needs of the Swarmers, who live their lives in the air.

Like a real city, the Swarm governs itself (through an airship oligarchy), trades with communities outside itself, accepts immigrants who meet its standards, and has persisted over generations. Reynolds is explicit: This is an "aerial city" where the protagonist Quillon, on arrival, hears "four thousand subtly different engine notes, not one tuned to exactly the same tone as any other, but combining, merging, threading, echoing off the crater walls to form one endless, throbbing, harmonically rich chorus that was utterly, shockingly familiar. The hum of the city."

The Swarm is a "distributed city," a concept that is emerging si-multaneously in urban planning theory and science fiction. The term can be derived by analogy from distributed computing where a single task is spread out among multiple networked but physically separate machines. A distributed city is one whose neighborhoods and districts are widely parceled out over space and form a unit by interacting over distance. It retains the spatial specialization of a normal city, but the pieces are scattered rather than adjacent.

A distributed city is not simply suburban sprawl, which is a phenomenon that we can map as a single contiguous geographic entity. Geographers and planners can debate where exactly to draw boundaries around metropolitan Toronto or Phoenix, but they agree that it can be done. A distributed city is something different. It can be mapped only as a discontinuous scattering of nodes or pieces that each play distinct roles as part of a larger whole.

There's really no distributed city yet to be found on our planetary surface. Megaregions like the BosWash megalopolis of the northeastern United States or Japan's Taiheiyo Belt (Pacific Belt) from Tokyo to Osaka and beyond might look at first glance like they fit the model—they consist of several nodes located along a corridor like beads on a string—but each component is fundamentally independent of the others.

Baltimore could exist without Philadelphia, Nagoya without Kobe, Portland without Seattle. The closest we have come in North America is the relationship Los Angeles and Las Vegas, which boomed in the later twentieth century as, in essence, a specialized recreational annex of LA separated by a hefty chunk of desert.

Another comparison are the "global cities" described by sociologist Saskia Sassen. She argues that the global economy has produced an interchangeable elite of corporate managers and financiers who inhabit the most expensive apartments and prestigious office buildings in New York, London, Tokyo, Paris, Hong Kong, Singapore, and Dubai and move with complete ease from one place to the next. Their "upper city" (think *Metropolis* here) is effectively a single place that happens to be distributed among several continents, given that the highest level .001 percent are at home anyplace their expensive wants and tastes can be satisfied. An example in contemporary fiction is the twenty-eight-year-old protagonist in Don Delillo's aptly titled *Cosmopolis,* an asset manager who spends the novel in a limousine between his Manhattan apartment and a haircutting salon while running a bet against the yen.

In urban theory circles, interest in distributed cities comes in part from concerns about urban survivability in the face of disasters like Hurricane Katrina and anticipation of the long term crisis of climate change. In response, a few planners have begun to explore the creation of resilient cities through massive decentralization that goes many steps beyond classic suburbanization. This is not nostalgic, anti-urban back-to-the-land thinking of the sort that permeates much of American culture and some of its science fiction (like Clifford Simak's *City*). It is about using the power of long-distance communication to create new urban forms.

The government of Scotland offers an example. A report by Design Innovation Scotland recently offered up the idea of distributed city as a new way to think about regional economic development. The report calls it an "imagined city" in which enterprises and communities across a large region (it suggests the Highlands and Islands) are linked laterally into a functioning whole that is greater than the sum of its parts. Thinking in these terms, the Scottish planners see a distributed city as a way in which "apparently disparate resources—intellectual, physical, social and material—can be usefully related to one another to create motivational, distributed enterprises within a regional ecology of cultural and economic activities." The economic development jargon from Edinburgh bureaucrats is a bit painful to read, but the idea is there.

Because the term is still in the process of settling firmly into urban planning, there are some alternative applications for "distributed city" that emphasize devolution from large-scale metropolitan systems to small-scale and localized planning. Australian environmentalist and "green urbanist" Peter Newman argues for a model of distributed cities in which energy systems, utilities, and transportation have been decentralized to avoid disastrous system-wide crashes—an idea that Stan Robinson embodied in *Pacific Edge* nearly a quarter century ago. Michael Blowfield and Leo Johnson in the brand new book *Turnaround Challenge: Business and the City of the Future* use "distributed city" to emphasize the importance of scattered, small-scale innovation nodes that can network from places as different as Nairobi and Austin. It is an appealing idea in its own right, but Cory Doctorow stole their thunder with his depiction of the New Work in *Makers* (2009).

We can understand the more radical sort of distributed city by revisiting *Terminal World,* where Reynolds contrasts the Swarm with Spearpoint, a vast towering city in the shape of a tapering cone that is home to 30 million people. Fifteen leagues across at its base, it narrows to one-third league across at fifty leagues above the ground and keeps rising into the vacuum.

Spearpoint represents the much more common science fiction type of the city as megastructure—the Urban Monads in Robert Silverberg's *The World Inside,* the self-contained moving cities in Greg Bear, *Strength of Stones,* or the huge block of Todos Santos in Larry Niven and Jerry Pournelle, *Oath of Fealty* (1981), which is a single arcology a thousand feet high and two miles on a side with enough floor area to overlay the entire five boroughs of New York.

Where these writers were imagining the ultimate coalescence of high-rise Manhattan or Chicago into a single accreted super-structure, the distributed city offers a sharp contrast with some new and innovative ways to think about urban futures in science fiction as well as urban planning.

Distributed cities do the science fiction work of upsetting the image and reality of cities as vast, fixed agglomerations that grow higher and wider as time passes. They embody the ability of science fiction to challenge basic economic and social assumptions.

The antecedent of the radically distributed city is a brief theoretical speculation by the early Soviet sociologist and planner Mikhail Okhitovich, who wrote in opposition to high modernist theorists of the high-rise city like Le Corbusier.

Associated with the radical Soviet architects of the Constructivism movement, Okhitovich in 1929 published a short article on "The Problem of the City" that proclaimed the idea of "disurbanism." With modern technology, he said, the new socialist society would not have to crowd together in the centralized capitalism city. His alternative was the Red City of the Planet of Communism—perhaps envisioned for Earth or perhaps as a socialist utopia for Mars in the tradition of Alexander Bogdanov's *Red Star* (1908).

The new city would be structured by social relations rather than territory, he argued, and the different functions of a city no longer needed to exist in one physical place. Instead, he wrote, "the whole world is at our service." He envisioned overlapping activity waves of greater and lesser intensity that would span the planet, sometimes overlapping and reinforcing to create a network of urban nodes that together constituted urban society.

Okhitovich himself ran afoul of Joseph Stalin and was executed in a gulag in 1937, plunging his ideas into official disrepute. Architectural historians in the 1980s resurfaced his work along with other advocates of the radical Soviet architectural theories of Constructivism. His ideas now make it into blogs on architecture and utopias.

The distributed cities that are now appearing in science fiction, with their indirect debt to Okhitovich, have yet to settle into a standard pattern. In a simple example, Iain M. Banks in *Surface Detail* uses the term "distributed city" for a set of supersized high-rise structures scattered over a planetary surface. It is as if the suburban "edge city" nodes described by journalist Joel Garreau were uprooted from their locations outside Washington and Houston and plopped randomly across a much wider landscape.

Jay Lake takes an opposite tack in imagining a distributed "Cascadiopolis" in the near-future Pacific Northwest. His story "Forests of the

Night" appears in the original anthology *Metatropolis*. The stories from other contributors such as Tobias Bucknell and editor John Scalzi take place in recognizable extrapolations of regular cities like Detroit and St. Louis, and their plots revolve around the classic tension between privilege and powerlessness in urban centers and peripheries.

Lake, in contrast, imagines an alternative city that weaves its way through the forests and mountains of the Cascade Range in the Pacific Northwest. His city consists of a networked set of isolated enclaves that look individually like forest compounds but together amount so something much more. As he said in a recent email, "it's not like I had a map or anything. Just visualizing a distributed, zero-footprint city environment spread out through lava tubes, tree platforms and low-impact temporary surface structures."

The refugee fleet that comes together in the re-imagined television series *Battlestar Galactica* is also a distributed city. It consists of several dozen physically distinct and sometimes quite distant units. Because series continuity was not always great, the number of ships at different times and in different episodes ranged variously around several dozen. There are big "neighborhoods" like *Galactica* with more than 2500 people and smaller ships with populations in the mid-hundreds. The total population of this discontinuous settlement totals just about 50,000, the size of a small city like Binghamton, New York or Grand Junction, Colorado.

Like cities with neighborhoods and districts, the fleet's individual ships specialize in particular activities that together make up a functioning city. There are cargo ships, mining ships (*Monarch*), industrial ships like the tylium refinery ship *Daru Mozu*, a hospital ship (*Rising Star*), a prison ship (*Astral Queen*), residential ships like *Cloud Nine,* a government center on *Colonial One,* and, of course, military ships like *Galactica.*

They function together, exchanging personnel and residents, sometimes shifting functions, and battling over politics. The fleet lacks the permanence of a real city, but for a few brief years it amounts to a city parceled out among vast reaches of space.

These are innovative ways to think about cities, which have always been grounded in very specific locales, but there is a precedent from 2450 years ago, as recounted from the Greek-Persian wars. William Adama had an ancestor in Themistocles, also the captain of a distributed city-fleet standing against the overwhelming might of an implacable enemy.

Here is what Herodotus reported about debates among the Greek leaders after Athens had fallen to the invaders:

When Themistocles thus spoke, the Corinthian Adeimantos inveighed against him for the second time, bidding him to be silent because he had no native land, and urging Eurybiades not to put to the vote the proposal of one who was a citizen of no city; for he said that Themistocles might bring opinions before the council if he could show a city belonging to him, but otherwise not. This objection he made against him because Athens had been taken and was held by the enemy. Then Themistocles said many evil things of him and of the Corinthians both, and declared also that he himself and his countrymen had in truth a city and a land larger than that of the Corinthians, so long as they had two hundred ships fully manned.

A distributed city highlights interrelations among the different parts of a great city—their simultaneous specialization and interaction. It also requires flexibility that is the opposite of a vast, stable arcology. A distributed city can grow by accretion and shrink by secession, like the Galactica fleet. Half a century ago, urban planner Melvin Webber proposed that the increasing power of communication technologies would allow "communities without propinquity." Webber was thinking of the loosened constraints of geography within metropolitan areas, but his idea of a "non-place urban realm" is excellent shorthand for distributed cities envisioned on much vaster scales. Planners and theorists are still coming to grips with the possibilities, and imaginative writers have an open invitation to step in and help.

ABOUT THE AUTHOR

Carl Abbott has taught urban studies and planning at Portland State University in five decades (not fifty years!). His interest in science fiction began with reading *Rocket Ship Galileo* in fourth grade and the much scarier *Star Man's Son: 2050 A.D.* in fifth grade. He has since written *Frontiers Past and Future: Science Fiction and the American West* (2006) and published several articles about science fiction in history and urban planning journals as well as in Science Fiction Studies, on topics as diverse Jack London, Kim Stanley Robinson, and cyberpunk cities. His current project is tentatively titled *Science Fiction Cities: Seven Ways We Image the Urban Future*.

Driving through a Cloud with Pat Cadigan

JEREMY L. C. JONES

© 2013 John O'Halloran
Ohana TyeDye Photography

Used to be that Pat Cadigan could "do anything in five thousand words or less," but these days she's running a little long. Her stories are bumping up closer to ten thousand. Not much else has changed. Her work remains relentlessly unpredictable, and simultaneously forward-looking and retro-flective.

It's been easiest for critics, reviewers, and fans to label Cadigan a cyberpunk writer and then offer a variety of caveats. Indeed, she has written and continues to write about the many and varied intersections of technology and biology, but once you try to put Cadigan in a category you rapidly find more exceptions to than confirmations of the rule.

Cadigan is driven to write.

"The same thing that compels me to live [compels me to write]," she said. "It's just what I do, and I'm always doing it, even if I'm not at the keyboard."

There is often an undercurrent of dark humor and the looming shadow of dark past in her fiction; occasionally there's even nagging feeling that someone is pulling one over on you while also being deadly serious.

Cadigan can dodge any bullet the future fires at humankind, it seems. She speculates around corners and sees into the shadows of even the darkest possibilities. Her vision of tomorrow is kaleidoscopic.

Author of the novels *Mindplayers, Synners,* and *Fools,* as well as numerous stories and novellas, Cadigan has been nominated numerous times for the Hugo but it wasn't until this year that she finally won the award, along with the Locus Award for the novelette "The Girl-Thing Who Went Out for Sushi." Orbiting Jupiter, humans opt to surgical modify themselves to be like marine lifeforms such as octopuses. She recently released a holiday story, "The Christmas Show." Additionally, "Chalk," tells a story of two friends who a private place to be creative away from the prying eyes of adults only to discover magic.

What do these stories all have common beyond their author? They're all different.

Is there ever a limit to the "exciting possibilities and dangerously unpredictable" aspects of writing?

The only limits are those the writer sets, either consciously or unconsciously. I am primarily a fiction writer but twenty years ago, I ran away with a carnival sideshow so I could write an article about it for *Omni* magazine. Well, I didn't *really* run away. I had been GOH at a convention in Calgary, Alberta, and they brought in Scott McClelland's Carnival Diablo to perform. It was wonderful. After the performance, I got to know Scott and the other performer Ryan Madden and we kept in touch.

Later that year, the sideshow had some dates to play in British Columbia and I decided that it would make a great article. So I pitched it to then-editor-in-chief Keith Ferrell, who gave me the go-ahead and I traveled with Scott and Ryan and Julianne Manchur who had joined the show. It was a total departure for me. Travelling through the Canadian Rockies in a van in December can be exhilarating but it can also be scary. I remember when we drove through a cloud—we were high up and the clouds were that low. I'd thought it would be like driving through a patch of fog but it was decidedly different. It wasn't an easy trip but I'd do it again in a heartbeat.

I've since written two nonfiction books—I lucked into an assignment to write the book about the making of the *Lost In Space* movie in 1997 and I was able to write it because I'd learned how to write nonfiction with Carnival Diablo. The next year, Universal re-made *The Mummy* and I was lucky enough to write the making-of book for that one, too. After the book came out, Mike Resnick told me I had done a very good job. I felt like I'd gotten an Olympic medal; Mike has traveled extensively in Africa and has forgotten more about Egypt than I'll ever learn.

And just FYI: I was in my mid-to-late forties when I took on those making-of assignments. You don't have to be a young person to try something new.

Are there any stories in which you feel as though you got it "wrong" or took a misstep? And, conversely, what are some of the stories that helped you turn corners or take leaps forward? And why?

Well, I had to make a late correction in the galleys of my first novel, *Mindplayers*. When I started the novel, there was no way to signal someone who was in the middle of REM sleep, to tell them they were dreaming, without waking them up. By the time I turned the novel in, a method had been developed to do that, so a person could receive a low-level stimulus to tell them they were dreaming, so they could dream lucidly—i.e., they know they're dreaming and they take charge of the action. I had to change that part of the novel in which I stated it wasn't possible.

Conversely, *Synners* isn't as science-fictional as it used to be. Some of the technology is now possible. The technology that isn't possible has not been proved to be impossible yet.

What are you working on now?

I'm working on the novel based on/inspired by/taking off from "The Girl-Thing Who Went Out For Sushi," working title: *See You When You Get There*. I also have several other novels simmering on the back-burner as well.

Without getting into content, how are you moving from "The Girl-Thing" to See You When? Are you adding on, launching off, what?

"Girl-Thing" will not be part of the novel, which occurs a few hundred years after.

How has it challenged you so far?

I've had to learn even more nuts-and-bolts about the solar system, interplanetary travel, habitats in space, and all kinds of other stuff I won't go into right now because I don't want to spoil the surprise.

How much of what you do just happens and how much is planned out beforehand?

That depends on what I'm working on. Sometimes an idea arrives whole; other times I have to write my way through it and keep slogging. When I work at novel-length, I always have a roadmap—I know where I'm starting out from and where I want to go, and I know the major milestones I'll hit in between. But it's not so mapped out that there won't be surprises. I like to leave room for spontaneous combustion/generation, not to mention the occasional detour/side-trip/scenic overlook.

You've been doing this now for a good while, has your process changed much? If so, how?

I've been a professional writer for thirty-four years; for the first thirty-three, I simply wrote whenever, however I could. These days, I lounge on the sofa with my iPad and my Bluetooth keyboard, often with the cat curled up on my lap and music playing. I start early in the morning and go until I'm dry. At some point in the late afternoon, I put on the TV, even if I'm still working. As the quintessential American teenager, I did all my homework in front of the TV and I still do.

After years of having built in time limits and restraints, responsibilities as a caregiver, how do you keep from just . . . you know, watching the TV without doing the writing?

All these years, I haven't been making time to watch TV, I've been making time so I can write. I'm never not connected to my writing. That's just how it works for me.

Is there a part of a story, long or short, that tends to give you the most difficulty?

Yes. There are difficulties inherent in every part of a story. Which will give me the most trouble depends on the story. They're all different. It just depends on the story.

Do you feel more at home in the short form or the long form?

For the last ten years, I've been writing short fiction because caring for my elderly mother was so demanding it was impossible to find enough time and space to think at novel-length. She passed away just before Christmas in 2012 and now I'm able to plan novels again.

The short story is my first love because that's where I started out. Well, technically, the novelette, according to SFWA word-counts. Back when I was working a full-time day job (and looking after a new baby), I could do anything in five thousand words or less. It was all I had time for. My first novel was actually a fix-up of a few novelettes and a short story, with added interstitial material—Shawna McCarthy, who was at Bantam then, had read the stories and thought they'd make a good book. My second novel, *Synners*, was actually the first novel I wrote from beginning to end without any pre-existing material (it sort of jumped off from my short story "Rock On," but the story wasn't part of the novel).

Since then, I've been wordier—my shortest fiction seldom runs much below eight thousand words, and it's usually closer to ten thousand words even after rigorous cutting. Ellen Datlow taught me how to trim the fat and kill my darlings. (Although I don't really kill them—I cut them and put them in an out-takes file. That way I can have my cake and eat it, too.)

Generally, the story, whatever it may be, tells me whether it's the start of a novel or a stand-alone piece of short fiction.

How do you KNOW?

That's one I can't answer. I don't know how I know. I recognize it when I see it.

"The Girl-Thing Who Went Out For Sushi," which won a Hugo in 2013, (please pardon my immodesty for bragging), was meant to be a one-off. It was only after it came out—in *Edge of Infinity*, edited by Jonathan Strahan—that I consciously began thinking about a novel.

I was definitely working outside my comfort zone with "Girl-Thing." I had never written this kind of story before and I had to do a lot of research to get all the nuts-and-bolts right. It was hard but it was also great fun figuring out what the characters could and couldn't do, what could and couldn't happen. These things are not a matter of opinion and I knew I had to be really careful because, as I have pointed out elsewhere many times in the past, science fiction readers are *smart.* If you don't know the difference between centripetal force and centrifugal force, if you don't know the difference between weight and mass, if you don't know how things like angular momentum, orbital resonance, and gravity boosts work, you'll look like a moron. The readers will tell you and you'll *feel* like a moron.

And incidentally, now I'm sixty. You're never too old to try something different or learn something new.

ABOUT THE AUTHOR

Jeremy L. C. Jones is a freelance writer, editor, and teacher. He is the Staff Interviewer for *Clarkesworld Magazine* and a frequent contributor to *Kobold Quarterly* and *Booklifenow.com.* He teaches at Wofford College and Montessori Academy in Spartanburg, SC. He is also the director of Shared Worlds, a creative writing and world-building camp for teenagers that he and Jeff VanderMeer designed in 2006. Jones lives in Upstate South Carolina with his wife, daughter, and flying poodle.

Another Word:
Will Aliens be Alien?
CRAIG DELANCEY

It's a common complaint against science fiction: the aliens aren't really alien. They're humans in disguise.

Often enough it's a fair observation, especially in film. No one finds the motives of Klingons or Yoda or ET inscrutable. But in our novels too, extraterrestrial intelligences often appear very human-like—indeed, they're even often humanoid in form. We typically encounter them not as beings with motives that are completely new to us, but rather as demonstrating extremes on familiar means (for example, being more war-like, or more intelligent, or more peaceful than your average human).

This familiarity is often a product of the demands of telling a tale. If an extraterrestrial intelligence is going to be a character in your novel, then the reader must understand it for the narrative to be compelling. If your alien is incomprehensible, then its mysteriousness will come to be a theme, which may not serve your narrative goals. It is for this reason that our best SF stories about inscrutable aliens are specifically about this inscrutability: it stands out as an impediment to action, demanding attention.

But set aside the demands of story telling, and implicit in the humans-in-disguise criticism is the claim that extraterrestrial intelligences would be very—perhaps incomprehensibly—strange to us. Which begs the question: is this right? Should we expect that the distance between our home worlds were a kind of distance between our conceptions of the universe? Will we have so little in common that we cannot find shared semantic ground?

Perhaps not. For all (or nearly all) the organisms of the universe will share this common history: they will have evolved. Evolution results in boundless complexity, expressed in wild varieties of forms and behaviors, but its basic principles are simple and universal. A population has variation in it, augmented periodically by mutation. Populations grow to carrying capacity, and the result is fierce competition for survival. Some individuals succeed better than others in this competition, and have more offspring. These offspring will live to carry on some of the beneficial traits of their progenitors.

Consider: few of us expect that unintelligent extraterrestrial organisms will be incomprehensible. We arrive on planet X, and certain organisms are building hives, others are eating the hive makers, others are rapidly moving away from the organisms that eat the hive makers.

We interpret these organisms readily, without hesitation: that organism is cooperating with kin; that organism is hunting; that organism is fleeing. But such an expectation is no small matter, because intelligent aliens will be organisms too. They will have an evolutionary history shared with the other organisms of their planet. And this will provide the foundation for their skills, their motivations, and ultimately their intelligence.

For all the complexity that arises in the details, the universals of evolution mean that all organisms will share certain features. They will have evolved in competition.

Helping kin will increase the likelihood of the helpful trait being spread in the population. Since intelligence is likely to result in control of the environment, it is likely to result in the adoption of a K-strategy, in which the organisms have fewer offspring and invest more time and resources into the survival of those offspring; and if the organisms adopt a K-strategy, then they will have a deep interest in the success of their offspring. These constraints, and thousands of others, will lead naturally to certain dispositions and motivations—including what we call emotions.

These include a readiness to cooperate but an eagerness to find and punish cheaters; a love for kin; and a host of motives to protect one's own offspring. Surely, these could provide a foundation for mutual understanding.

There is an interesting parallel here with a debate in paleontology. The question concerns what Steven J. Gould called "running the tape over." He argued that if we could repeat the history of Earth over and over, allowing variations where they naturally occur, we would see wildly different outcomes across these different histories.

The alternative theory, championed most notably by Simon Conway Morris, is that evolution is more rigorously optimizing than this. On Conway Morris's account, history of life on Earth would have to produce bipedal, bilaterally symmetric intelligent beings after about as much time as it took for us to show up (accounting for events like asteroids falling on us, and re-setting the clock). Evolution, on this view, is highly constrained. It will reliably result in similar outcomes for similar conditions.

This debate about "running the tape over again" may represent two extremes to how difficult it will be to understand an extraterrestrial intelligence. I suspect Gould would have thought that extraterrestrial intelligences would be quite understandable, if we could just know something about their evolutionary history. But for him, the greater disparity of possible evolutionary outcomes would mean that extra work will be required to discern the evolutionary constraints that are relevant to a species.

On the other hand, the more optimal evolution turns out to be, the more readily identifiable we can expect the foundation for mutual understanding to be. If an organism's strategy is best for its environment, and any old starting place will get its lineage there, then this should hold true for an extraterrestrial in a similar environment.

We might expect the alien to have eyes, recognizable as like our eyes, because we expect that eyes like our own are a relatively effective way to seize the benefits of visual perception. We might expect the alien to have an analog of fear, since a general motivation to avoid predators and other dangers, and remember them as threatening, appears to be a very effective. And so on.

The heritage of a single organism is one thing. Cultures are another. We are well familiar with failures of human beings to understand each other. Surely the situation will be worse with respect to an extraterrestrial culture. Culture adds something new, something that changes quickly and varies widely across individuals of a single genotype. Won't this make our extraterrestrials incomprehensible?

The case of human cultural variation is easily exaggerated. We tend to focus upon differences, but the fact remains that no matter how alien a human culture, it remains possible to understand much of it. We read the *Illiad* or the *Mahabarata* or the *Popul Vuh*, and though the writers of those works are far from some of us in time and space, we find nothing incomprehensible in the motives and actions of their protagonists.

Culture builds upon what evolution provides. In language and customs we find explosive variety. But these varieties are less successful, and more difficult to maintain, precisely to the degree that they oppose what evolution has instilled in the species.

Culture adds complexity, but it cannot (at first, anyway) extinguish the goals and motives we inherit. You can ask that your warriors not fear death, but we can predict that they normally will.

This allows us to make a modest prediction. Extraterrestrial intelligences will resist understanding to the degree that their culture is complex. Nothing about their evolutionary history would be incomprehensibly strange to us, and thus nothing about the motives and abilities that they inherit would be incomprehensibly strange to us. Rather, what will allow for strangeness is the ways in which intelligence and culture take those basic motives and combine and reformulate them into surprising new forms. Aliens will have an evolutionary history like those we find here on Earth, and surprising cultural complexity to alter and reinterpret and redirect the abilities and motives that this history gave them. That means a biological understanding can serve as the basis for cultural understanding. We have a Rosetta Stone: it's called Darwinism.

So extraterrestrial intelligences won't be humans in disguise. But they'll be something quite similar to that: they'll be an evolutionary history, dressed up in culture.

Now, if only they'd call us.

ABOUT THE AUTHOR

Craig DeLancey is a philosopher and writer. His novels include *Gods of Earth*, available from 47North Press. His short stories include "Julie is Three," which won the Anlab reader's choice award and has been reprinted, in translation, in Russia and China. He also writes plays, and his plays have had performances and staged readings in New York, Sydney, Melbourne, and in other cities. He has been a finalist for the Heideman Award. He teaches philosophy at the State University of New York at Oswego.

Editor's Desk:
Anthologies, Patreon, and the 2013 Reader's Poll & Contest

NEIL CLARKE

Happy New Year!

If you are new to the *Clarkesworld* family, you may not know that we also publish an annual anthology series that collects all the original fiction published over the course of a year. The first two volumes went by the name *Realms 1* and *2*, but since then they've carried the *Clarkesworld* name. The print editions look great on your bookshelf, but the ebook editions are good too.

Our latest volume, *Clarkesworld: Year Five,* was released just before the holidays. (Yes, we are a bit behind, but have been making a valiant effort to get caught up.) At present, *Year Six* is scheduled for the end of the first quarter and *Year Seven* is on-track for release at Readercon in July.

Working on these volumes has been a fun look back at some of the amazing stories our authors have written for us over the years. I hope you all consider purchasing one or more. Every penny made from these volumes goes back into our fiction budget.

Read about our anthologies here:
clarkesworldmagazine.com/staff/#realms

Have you heard of Patreon?

Patreon is best described as a cross between Kickstarter and subscriptions. Instead of focusing on a big project, like a book or a movie, Patreon is for people who produce recurring content, like podcasts, YouTube channels, web comics, or a magazine. Patrons make pledges to give a monthly amount for each month that new content is released. Similar to Kickstarter, there are community giving goals and individual rewards for your support.

To make ends meet, we sell our books and electronic subscriptions, but over the years, people have repeatedly asked for other alternatives to support us financially. To that end, we've established a Patreon page and just like our promise to increase the number of stories we publish when we hit a specific subscriber count, we've added a similar goal to our Patreon page. We could have two additional stories per issue if both of these goals are met and as I mentioned previously, it would only take a small percentage of our readers/listeners to get us there.

Check out our Patreon page at:
www.patreon.com/clarkesworld

January means it's time for our annual *Clarkesworld* Reader's Poll. Each year, we ask our readers to pick their favorite cover art and original stories from the past year. Here's a quick list to refresh your memory:

Fiction

- "Driftings" by Ian McDonald
- "Variations on Bluebeard and Dalton's Law Along the Event Horizon" by Helena Bell
- "Effigy Nights" by Yoon Ha Lee
- "Gravity" by Erzebet YellowBoy
- "The Wanderers" by Bonnie Jo Stufflebeam
- "Vacant Spaces" by Greg Kurzawa
- "The Weight of a Blessing" by Aliette de Bodard
- "The Last Survivor of the Great Sexbot Revolution" by A.C. Wise
- "86, 87, 88, 89" by Genevieve Valentine

Cover Art

The small versions of the art on the following pages hardly does them justice. You can find full-sized versions on our website at:

clarkesworldmagazine.com/artgallery

"Winding Down" by Alex Ries

"Concrete 9" by Yang Xueguo

"The Emperor's Arrival" by David Demaret

"The Awakening" by Alexandru Popescu

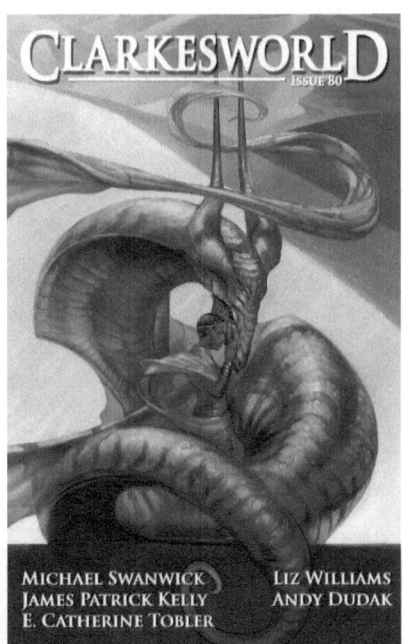

"Desert Dragon" by Julie Dillon

"Rainforest God" by David Melvin

"The Land of Lost Dreams" by Dan Osborne

"Launch Point" by Julie Dillon

"Silent Oracle by Matt Dixon

"Neo Maya" by Raúl Cruz

"Lost in Space" by Piotr Foksowicz

"Elliptic" by Julie Dillon

To participate, visit:

clarkesworld2013.questionpro.com

Please fill in the optional name and email address questions if you'd like to be entered into a contest where you can win either one of three copies of *Clarkesworld: Year Five* or, for one lucky winner, the complete 2013 print run of *Clarkesworld*.

Our survey is open now and will continue through February 10th, 2014. Winners will be revealed in our March 2014 issue.

ABOUT THE AUTHOR

Neil Clarke is the editor of *Clarkesworld Magazine,* owner of Wyrm Publishing and a 2013 Hugo Nominee for Best Editor (short form). He currently lives in NJ with his wife and two children.

Cover Art:
Guten Morgen
WALDEMAR KAZAK

Russian artist **Waldemar Kazak** has worked as a book and packaging designer for many years. While designing beer cans, he became hooked on drawing with a graphics tablet. He loves to incorporate a touch of irony, but never hate, into the characters he draws and often features 60s-70s retro elements in his settings.

WEBSITE

waldemarkazak.com